Just for You!

‖‖ ‖ ‖ ‖ ‖‖‖‖‖ ‖‖‖‖ ‖‖ ‖ ‖‖‖
I0563043

The Song

HIS MOTHER SINGS

Teresa Collins

AUTHOR CONTACT INFORMATION
Teresa Collins
teresac0555@gmail.com
815-483-8435

ACKNOWLEDGEMENTS

ATO Publishing (And They Overcame)
Founder: Teresa Collins

Cover Layout & Design:
Wow Factor Studios - 815-483-8435

Editorial Director:
David Collins

Assistant Editorial Director:
Claudia Cox

Pre-publication Content Review and Feedback:
Terrance Patillo
Dwayne Collins
Eric Patillo
Joslyn Collins
Trent Collins

Musical References:
"Lord Don't Move My Mountain" by Inez Andrews
"Pass Me Not Oh Gentle Savior" by Fanny Crosby
"Day N Night" by Kid Cudi

Keynote Scripture:
Come unto me, all ye that labour and are heavy laden, and I will give you rest. Take my yoke upon you, and learn of me; for I am meek and lowly in heart: and ye shall find rest unto your souls.
JESUS CHRIST – Matthew 11:28-29

Poetic Contributions
"If We Must Die" by Claude McKay

Scriptural References:
AKJV of The Word Of God

Dedication

This composition is dedicated to everyone who knows the pain of parent abuse, and to those who are willing to share their story to help others rise above it.

[28] Come unto me, all ye that labour and are heavy laden, and I will give you rest. [29] Take my yoke upon you, and learn of me; for I am meek and lowly in heart: and ye shall find rest unto your souls. [30] For my yoke is easy, and my burden is light. Matthew 11:28-30 AKJV

CONTENTS

Prologue

There's nothing like that first leak of the day. Nobody told me that my whole body would become a slave to it.

I'm lying in bed like a dead man, and out of nowhere, my eyes pop open. I wake up under pressure, mumbling, "Who are you?" Then I look down and realize that I have a fireman's hose in my boxers, and it's full throttle. My bladder is on the very verge of voluntarily violating my rights as a man and owner of my body. I can feel the ferocious stream surging unapologetically against the tiny opening of the nozzle.

But I stay calm.

It's all slow-motion.

I have done this a thousand times

for the past 17, almost 18 years...

Wake up, take a deep sigh, look at cell phone:

2:03 A.M. on the dot.

Mutter some dumb stuff about almost wetting my draws.

Roll out of bed.

Feet fall onto the cold floor.

Scratch balls.

Tighten sphincter muscle to avoid a leak.

Walk straight, then left, then straight again.

No light is needed for this voyage.

I can do it with closed eyes, with or without the shy slither of illumination shining through the foyer window.

Enter bathroom.

Position myself squarely in front of the toilet and aim for the hole in the middle of the bowl.

Don't ask me why; I just do.

It's art.
I've done it this way every single morning for as long as I've been doing it this way every single morning…
Place cell phone on sink.
Stick out left arm,
Press left hand on wall behind toilet.
Lean forward.
Try not to miss.
Hold my junk with right hand.
"Man, my aim is off."
Turn and adjust.
GOT IT.
Tilt head forward.
Close eyes.
Now pee.
Swoooooooooole…
Winding down as the pressure lifts.
Swooooop… swoop… drip… drip… drip.
"Aaaaah."
Feeling 10 gallons lighter.
Open eyes.
Shake twice,
Squeeze once.
Anything more, you on some other stuff, bruh.
Reel hose back into fire truck.
Flush.
Turn to sink.
Turn on water.
Briskly run junk hand through water for precisely one quick second.
No soap required.

It's just the politically correct thing to do.
"Did you wash your hands?"
"Yuuup."
Dry hands on boxers.
Grab phone.
Walk through foyer.
Straight, then right, then straight again.
Mind racing.
Busy day ahead.
Glance at cell phone:
2:05 A.M., on the dot.
Left eye barely open.
Right, completely closed.
It's been a long night.
Plop onto bed, face down.
Sleep like a dead man.

Business is dope. It's 12:48 A.M., and I have two more stops to make in this fancy pants, whitecoat community.

Where I'm from is not all fancy, but it's not a shabby gig either. But this... this is definitely an enormous upscale reclassification... a real Beverly Hills 90210-201 type situation. It's the kind of community clogged with a crapload of overachieving men who love to tout their wonderful, ill-gotten conveniences. They marquee their anorexic wives, go sailing on Saturday afternoons, enjoy long walks in the park, visit the museum of art and hang expensive paintings on their hubristic walls. Instead of going to church on Sunday mornings, they host pricy pool parties. It's the kind of community where more than two children per household is a glorified family complication, and when a wife, or wife's daughter, has a "miscarriage," that's code for "private abortion with a midwife." But hey, they're all pro-choice, right? There's no litter in sight, not so much as a lottery ticket, but then again, it's nightfall in this Listerine-swished cavity of a town.

I see trash going in and out of these lavish office buildings all day when I'm conducting my business. Trash cleans up nicely during the day. Put a suit and tie on it, spritz it up with some fancy backroom law degree, a few bribes and payoffs... then fan your hand around briskly to clear all the phony celebratory hoopla and "Voila`!"

There are definitely those who consider me trash. There's always that small, highfaluting margin who does. Even my clients... they choose these dead-man hours, not me. And even if their neighbors or business partners don't know, I do. Some of them run in the same circles, but I'm

2

not here to judge. I'm here for one purpose only: to collect that paper... advance my personal financial agenda. Why else would I be in this convoluted part of town? Everyone has an angle. And if your aim is off, you turn and make the proper adjustment. It's their right if they choose to hide me behind the still of the night, and do business with me using a collection of laminated discretions. I understand the hollow thoughts that rise up from their echoing hearts. Their souls are emptier than mine, desperately searching for a home, a meaningful purpose, one that is sincere, transparent, and artless. They work tirelessly to cork those hollows with those things... those privileges they take... those lies they tell themselves... and those Benjamin bloated deliveries I make.

I see through the whitewash and mental sludge they cover their truth in. It's a flyer stapled onto a tree at the park. It's a public service announcement. It's the same pretentious costume worn by all the colorful storytellers in their privileged villages. Their overuse of it has reduced its criminal arcanum to something as accessible as an ATM. No need to dress for the occasion. It is as casual as the flipflops they flounce around in at home or when shopping for dinner at the local Whole Foods Market – as long as they have their manufactured credentials tucked away in the hidden compartments of their soft leather wallets. It's a hard sale, but the justice system buys it – cha-ching. It's a signature mark of theirs. They are dirty marks playing a dirty game in a dirty world, deluded by dirty deals and deadly payoffs while drowning in deadly doses of hard liquor to wash down a dirty conscience...

My last stop is a top-heavy whitecoat in a quiet, well-kept condominium near the corner. I park exactly where I am told, about 12 miles south, under a heavily leafed row of trees where the street lights are shrouded by the leaves.

Obviously, I have a death wish or kahunas the size of sweet potatoes and bold enough to play Russian roulette in this genteel section of town.

The exchange is made without words, pleasantries, feelings, emotions, commitment, guilt or eye contact. There are no 'thank yous' or 'goodbyes'. She drives away as if I don't exist in her world and as if this passionate, discretionary moment in her life between us doesn't occur methodically, like clockwork, every Monday and Thursday.

I sit still and try not to move. But I get that nagging feeling... I look at my dash, it's 2:03 A.M. on the dot.

I exit my vehicle and take the six steps forward which leaves me standing face to face with a bright red fire hydrant on the corner, still shrouded by trees planted next to a swanky townhouse. I decide that this is the night that me and my little red friend will both put out fires. And seriously, it doesn't bother me to piss on or piss off a world that doesn't give a crap about me anyway.

I grabbed my angry snozzle and shot fury all over my little red friend. He had nothing to say. I shook twice, squeezed once and walked away from that sterile corner, and eased into my car with another successful heist under my belt. And seriously, this part of my work is almost as good as the money.

4

I turned up my music and drove away just like that whitecoat... without words, pleasantries, feelings, emotions, commitment, guilt or eye contact.

Uh, uh, uh, uh
Uh, uh
Day and night (what, what)
I toss and turn, I keep stressing my mind, mind
(what, what)
I look for peace but see I don't attain (what, what)
What I need for keeps this silly game we play, play
Now look at this (what, what)
Madness to magnet keeps attracting me, me
(what, what)
I try to run but see I'm not that fast (what, what)
I think I'm first but surely finish last, last
'Cause day and night (day and night)
The lonely stoner seems to free his mind at night
(night)
He's all alone through the day and night (day and night)
The lonely loner seems to free his mind at night
(at, at, at night)
Day and night (day and night)
The lonely stoner seems to free his mind at night
(night)
He's all alone. Some things will never change
(never change)
The lonely loner seems to free his mind at night
(at, at, at night)

Forty-five minutes later, I plop down on my own bed face down and sleep like a dead man...

***
Aaron, Are You Up?

The devil is always tampering around in my head, pushing those same old buttons, trying to get an ornery rise out of me. As always, he whispers a seemingly harmless thought, then falls back and waits for his poison to take effect.

"It's garbage day, honey," I hear her annoying voice reminding me.

"It's also barely 6 A.M.! Leave me alone! I'm tired." My eyes are still closed, but I can feel them beginning to twitching. "Man, you get on my nerves. I'mma kill you one day!"

Instead of jumping up like I am her puppet or something, rushing to take the garbage out, I continued lying there squeezing my eyes tighter and tighter trying to drown out her annoying nagging. I thought about the lizard I saw last week chillin' at the edge of the driveway, right where I usually drag both garbage cans.

"Aaron," her high-pitched voice rang again, methodically like an automated timer, over and over from the bottom of the staircase, around the banister, past the bathroom, the linen closet, and guest bed and bath and right into my man cave.

"You are going to miss the garbage pickup if you don't take the garbage out now, honey. Come on down these stairs."

I yawned and stretched out my arms and legs, like that dried-out lizard on the ground. His guts had that rainbow glow under the glare of the morning sun all week long, even after they became hard and crusty looking like fungated toenails.

Flattened by the trauma of the heavy square heel of my steel toe Timberlands, my chest pounded in excitement as I lay there in bed wondering if that lizard felt his spongy body collapse like a flat tire, or if he heard his tiny skull crack to pieces as my size 12-1/2s smashed it to smithereens.

It wasn't just the devil encroaching upon my thoughts. It was her...

"Aaron, honey. It's time to get up! Aaron!"

"Man, lady! Stop yelling. I hear you, with your annoying voice," I shouted grumpily, while kicking my legs in agitation. *The walls in this house are way too thin.* "Your voice is irritating! Stop calling my name!" *If she doesn't leave me alone, she is going to be next to hear her skull crack beneath my Timberlands. That lizard was just practice. She doesn't know how close I came to knocking her out last week – just keep messing with me, you old bitty!*

"Aaron! Honey!"

"I'm not listening to you, lady!"

"Do you hear me, honey?"

I hear her tiny feet shuffling away from the staircase and back into the kitchen. She was rushing, trying to flip the pancakes before they burned. She knows I love it when my pancakes are browned to perfection on both sides. And she knows what will happen to her if they are not.

"Ooooowee! She has it smelling like a premium-style pancake house in here! I can't wait to sink my teeth into them delicious cakes," I mumbled hungrily as I flipped over in bed, licking my lips and readjusting my pillow, preparing to take another catnap before I immerse myself into my awaiting dining ecstasy.

Like clockwork, she shuffled back to the bottom of the staircase.

"Aaron, come on, honey. It's 20 minutes after 7:00 A.M. Are you up? You know it's hard for you to get up when you don't have enough rest! And you didn't turn that TV off again. It was on all day. I was calling up the stairs for over an hour before I finally gave up. And what time did you get home last night? I didn't hear you come in."

"Didn't you just hear me say, 'stop talking to me'? I heard you, but you are not listening to me. I am ignoring you, lady. I turned it off when I turned it off. And as far as getting home. I got home when I got home. Now shut up!"

She called up the stairs again, "Aaron, do you hear me, baby? Come on downstairs!"

"Why do you do this to me? I'm not trying to see your face first thing in the morning. I have enough nightmares as it is. What makes you think I want to wake up to a horror show every day?"

"Aaron? Do you hear me? And don't complain about being tired. You stayed up half the night!"

She always has something to get on me about. And she always has a smart-aleck, disrespectful comment, no matter how I answer her. Who cares about what time I turn the TV off and on? Bothering me about that dumb TV! "It's my TV! I turn it off when I'm ready to turn it off! I pay all the bills up in here. She hates me. That's why she does this. Well, at least we have it in common. I hate her, too! I can't stand her and that squeaky voice she has. I jumped out of bed and opened and slammed my bedroom door again and again, hoping to get on her very last nerve.

"What's going on up there, Aaron? Are you ok?"

"Ugh. You are so irritating," I yelled while rushing back to my bed, squirming around in it briskly, trying to pull the covers over my head and block out her blabbing! *Where is my cell phone? Man! I'm always misplacing that thing.* I'm scrambling around the bed, trying to feel for it in between the sheets or blanket. *Hmmm, not there. Man, I need to clean this room up! It's a cave today, for sure.* I push around the pile of junk on my nightstand, and there it is, beneath a pair of my lightly worn underwear! *Her sorry but can't even wash my draws. I don't know why I keep her around. It's time for her to go.*

"AARON! Get out of that bed, honey. I don't hear any moving around up there! AARON anymore. Did you get back in bed!"

"Shut up, please shut up!"

***

Gap!
CELL PHONE RINGS

"Gap," I say. "What up, bro!"

"What's up Ace?" Gap said. "Where you at! You still coming through or what?"

"Come on, bro. Chill out with all that. I'm on my way!"

"What's taking you so long? You late, bro!"

9

"Nah bro, I'm never late. You know how I do. I'm like a chameleon. I'm switching things up. Can't have eyes on me like that, bro. I got everything set at the spot already – a whole wardrobe and everything, bro. We good."

"Well, what time will you get here, Ace?"

"Soon, Gap. My OG is in the kitchen whipping me up some grub. I gotta do this little breakfast thang with her... You know how it go."

"Bro..., you are so lucky. These tricks my dad bring through here be trying to push up on me more than they push up on him, fa' real. I love coming over to your house. Your mom is cool as Kool-Aid, bro. She cooks for your grown butt and everythang. I miss her cooking, too. Your mom can throw down in the kitchen, Ace. I haven't been there in a minute, though. My dad's tricks don't do nothing, straight up. Can I get a plate, my brotha? Whatever she cooking, I'm eating. Straight like that!"

"Nah bruh! The kitchen closed to sensitive brothers today, bro. How you gon' be hungry and sensitive all at the same time. Kitchen closed! Now, what you can do is bring your old self over here and put in some work, punk. How many times do a brother got to feed you? I done already put you on, punk. Now, put your chef hat on. Moms can use a lil' help. She slippin' bro. But cooking is yo' thang. Plus, you look good in an apron, bro. Soft niggas always do; looking all Cutthroat Kitcheny. Don't even front."

"Nah, bro. You got jokes; I see."

"Nah, I'm serious, bro. I know you like a Master Magician in the kitchen or something. You can make anything taste good! You need to have like your own restaurant or something, bro, facts.

"Ok, that's love, bro. But before the restaurant, just tell moms to hook me up. I want me some real home cooking, bro. Just save me a piece of sausage or a biscuit or something. Yeah, and tell her to fix me a bowl of grits. The kind where she puts all those shrimps and green onions in them. Man! Them joints is good! I feel like smashing right now! Seriously, bro. Ask your mom to hook a brother up! Fix me a plate!"

I told you, bro. No charity. Like my mom always say, "If a man don't work, he shouldn't even think about going in the kitchen. And what is you, life fifty? And still waiting on yo' moms to cook? Nah, brah. Nah. Bring yo' apron and come wash these dishes, bro!"

"Bro, you trippin' today..."

Momma yells up the stairs again, "Aaron! Come eat your breakfast, honey. It's almost time for you to go to school."

Gap hears her voice over the phone and says, "Oh snap. Is that her? Is that your moms I hear? I forgot how sweet her voice sounds! I ain't seen her in like forever! What's up, Momma! Heeey Beautiful! How you doing this morning, Ma? Put me on the speaker, bro!"

"Yeah, man, that's her. But gon' somewhere with all that mushy stuff. I'm not letting that fool touch my phone. Ain't no telling where her hands been, bro. But, hold up, let me shut this fool up..."

"I'm not going to school, fool!" I yelled at Momma. "STOP CALLING ME! GO AWAY! GO HARASS SOMEONE ELSE! PLEASE."

"BROOO," Gap yells, "What's wrong with you? You foul, bro. How do you talk to your mom like that? You have a good moms. I'm telling you, bro. You are wrong for that, Ace. You wrong. You should give your moms more respect than that. I'm just saying."

"I'm just saying, too, bro. She is sooo irritating. I'm getting ready to go down there and slap her again! Last time I slapped her cripple face down to the floor. And all she did was lay down there crying, looking at me like I cared. Fool! I'm the one that knocked you down there! What you looking up at me for? I ain't got no love for you! Cripple, no walking self. Shut up!"

"Ace, bro! Do you hear yourself?"

"What, fool? You don't know that lady, man. She foul, bro. She's down there at the bottom of the stairs yellin' at me right now, cursing me out and everything! She's a real douche bag, bro. I'm telling you, she irritating!"

"Ace, stop frontin'. Your mom is not cursing you out. She don't even curse, bro. Your mom is real sweet. You need to check yourself, bro. That's moms you dissin', bro. You ain't got but one. Not like me, bro. I get a new mom every time my pops walk through the door. Fa' real."

"Gap, you wild. Your pops be on the honeys, just like the honey is on them nuts and Cheerios! He's still a playa', with his crazy self. He still be talking all reckless?"

"Yeah, bro. But I'm not on that right now. I'm talking about your mom, bro. You kind of reckless for how you coming at her, bro. Word."

"Chill bro. You don't know my moms like that. She got all of y'all fooled, bro. She's down there threatening to put me out right now. Got a knife in her hand, threatening to cut me. Talking about she is going to call the po-po on me if I don't get my black, ashy behind down those stairs right now…. Listen to her. You hear that lil' high-pitched, squealing cat mouth down there? That's what I deal with every morning! I ought to go down there and slap her blind. She can't see as it is. She'll shut her mouth quick then."

"Ace, stop! You taking this too far, bro. I don't understand you. I hear none of what you are saying. Put the phone on speaker…"

"Whatever, bro. I can't believe you asked me to put that lady on my speaker, but whatever! Let me get off this phone so she don't call the po-po on me again. She pulls that crap every three or four days. I ought to break her phone again. Make her pay that expensive deductible to get it fixed. The dummy. Up here on a fixed income. My mom is stupid, bro. You don't know what it's like living with a dummy."

Momma yells up the stairs again, "Aaron, do you hear me, baby? You only have 30 minutes left before you have to leave. I don't want you to be hungry. Come on, honey. Breakfast is important… Can you hear me?"

"See, listen to her, bro. I told you. She is down there screaming and hollering at the top of her lungs. She sweating and cutting herself and everything. She out of control. I'm scared bro. That's why I always do her like I do. She acting like I stole some meat out of her freezer. Don't nobody want that old freezer-burned mess. Can you believe her, bro? She has a big chain wrapped around the refrigerator to lock me out of it. I got to go through 3 combination locks just to get a bottle of water. This is like prison, bro. One day, I'mma knock her out. You watch. I'mma knock her cold out and stuff her body in the freezer, bro."

"Aaron, honey, you up, baby? And the garbage man is gone. You missed him. But come on, I don't want you to miss breakfast."

"Ace... come on, bro, I know yo' moms..."

"But for real, Gap. I'm just messing with you, bro. She can't hear me. I would never talk to my mom that way. It's something with the acoustics in this house. It's like I'm in a sound vacuum or something. I can hear her, but she can't hear a word that comes out of my mouth. Plus, I think that old lady needs a hearing aid, too. It looks like one of her ears don't even have a hole in it. She looks retarded, bro. The entire hole is closed up on that joint. Her eardrums be on silent mode like all the time. All I know is she can't hear me," I said while laughing at her. Gap did not laugh with me.

"Gap, man, there you go, bro... being all sensitive... It's too early in the morning to be sensitive! I'm telling you, bro, that old lady can't hear me. See, watch this... Momma! Momma! MOMMAAAA! Old Lady! Stop yelling up these stairs at me every morning, fool. And even when I do decide to answer you, you can't hear a word I say. Stop yelling up here, dummy-you empty headed scarecrow." Gap didn't respond to me.

"Gap, you there," I ask. "Gap? So, what? You on silent mode, too... Gap! You there?"

"Yeah, I'm here, dawg. I don't know how to take you right now. You out here trippin' on your moms for nothing. Your moms ain't got nothing but love for you. And you over there tearing her down... You straight bogus for that."

"Gap! Come on, bro. You are starting to sound like my mom! And I told you, I'm never late, bro. I'm switching things up. Can't have too many eyes on me."

"Whatever, bro. Just come on so we can make this money, with your disrespectful self. You better cherish your moms, bro. You only get one. Out."

"Whatever, bro. I'm on the way. Out."

***

Yawning and stretching because I am still tired. Momma is right. I don't do well when I don't get enough rest. These dead man hours are killing me.

"Welp, ain't nothing to it but to do it." I can't believe I am quoting my mom right now! Ewww. I hate that hag! Gap has messed up my whole day. I ain't thinking about that lady. But let me get down these stairs and eat, then go pick up that fool."

"Aaron! You coming down? HONEY?"

"AAAVIAAA!" I yell extremely loudly into her ears. She jumps and grabs her chest. "Why are you yelling at me, Avia? I'm right here, stupid! Man!"

She looks over her shoulder from where she stood by the stove and smiles. "Boy, what have I told you about calling me by my name? That is disrespectful in this house. I am your mother."

"Yeah, yeah. I know. I'm just messing with you, **AAAVIAAA**." I snicker because I know she doesn't like it when I disrespect her. But I like getting on her nerves just because she gets on mine. She's always riding me and telling me to straighten up and fly right. I ain't no airplane.

She shakes her head and waves me off with her hand. "Boy, go on somewhere. You know you scared me a minute ago! I didn't hear you come down the stairs!"

"That's because you are deaf, Avia. You are always yelling. I can't even hear myself think in this house! Do you know that you sound like a mouse?" She waves me off with her hand and smiles again.

I mock her again. "Aaron, Aaron." I squeak in that same mousy, high-pitched tone, then crack up laughing and tell her she sounds retarded.

She waves me off again.

"So, how did you sleep, baby? That's if you slept at all. How many times must I remind you to turn that television off? A young man needs his rest, Aaron."

"Leave me alone, Momma! I'm not a child. I'm a grown man. Stop babying me," I said while rubbing the sleep from my eyes and hand brushing the wrinkles out of my shirt.

"Aaron, look at you, child! This is what I am saying. I know you are not about to leave this house looking like that. It looks like you slept in those clothes!"

"I did, aaand?"

"You are wrinkled from head to toe! At least let me iron your shirt, baby."

"Gon' Avia! Leave me ALONE! There's nothing wrong with my clothes! The ladies like me. They can't get enough of my loving!" I did a pelvis bump right in front of her and laughed in her face. She looked up toward the ceiling and sighed heavily...

"Come on, Momma, calm down. You can't take a joke. No body want none of what you got!"

Avia was on a roll today with waving me off with her hand. I couldn't do anything but laugh at her... looking like a broke down slave ship shuffling around the kitchen like she doesn't want ole Massa to sell her off at the auction.

"I cooked your favorite breakfast today... Blueberry pancakes with maple and honey smoked bacon."

"I'm not hungry."

"Oh, sit yourself down and shush your mouth, child. All your sassing!"

"You don't exist, Momma," I said and continued pressing the wrinkles out of my shirt while walking in the direction of that delicious, sweet-berry aroma oozing lusciously from the stove. I grabbed one of those gigantic, nine-inch plate-size, fluffy pancakes and devoured it in all of two bites. My jaws were poked out as far as the east is from the west... chewing and swallowing, oooing and aaahing. "Mmm, mmm, mmm." *This is definitely the one thing you always get right, Momma! Awww yeah. I'm about to smash now!*

As always, they were perfectly hot, fluffy, buttery, and browned to perfection, with just the right number of fresh blueberries in every bite!

"Mmm. These are on point," I mumbled.

"What did you say, Aaron? Did I hear you say something?" she asked with pleasure in her voice.

"Go away, Momma. You know I am not messing with you today." I turned my face a little farther away from her to block her from seeing the look of delicious satisfaction sliding across my entire face and head. "Plus, it's too early in the morning to talk to you. You don't have your thoughts together yet. You know it takes all day for your little bird brain to kick into gear. How are we going to conversate when you don't know what you want to say yet?"

"Boy hush," she said playfully. "I see you over there child licking your fingers. You can't hide those over-stuffed cheeks poking out on the sides of your face."

I ignore her again.

"And why did you have to stuff the whole pancake in your mouth like that?" she asked while laughing at me.

"You never could resist my blueberry pancakes! I knew you'd enjoy them! Now, go on to the table, and let me fix your plate."

What I wanted to say back to her was: "Because they are so good, Momma. That's why I stuffed the whole thing in my mouth. I can't get enough of them. These pancakes melt in your mouth. All these years, and you still get it right every single time! You are the best, Momma!"

But instead, I looked at her with disdain, rolled my eyes and headed toward the table. "These pancakes are alright, I guess. They are nothing to brag about. This is how you always fix them. Actually, they are a little dry. I feel like I am about to be sick. And frankly, if you ask me, you need to try a new recipe or something. I'm tired of these! And these blueberries taste like the freezer. You know I only eat fresh blueberries. You can't even get this right!"

I cut my eyes slightly in her direction to see what kind of reaction I would get out of her. She had a bigger-than-life, Sugar-Frosted-Flakes grin plastered all over her face. *Man! She knows I'm lying. I can't stand you, lady!*

"Yeah, ok," she said. "So, how many do you want, five or six?"

"Momma, please. Why are you buggin'? I already told you, these pancakes are nasty. I'm choking right now. I don't want any."

"Alright! Suit yourself! But I hate to see them go to waste!"

"Man, Avia! You just can't leave me alone! But since you keep riding me, just give me four or five more. Nah, make it six. Man, you get on my nerves."

"Six," she chuckled! "Coming right up!"

"And, you may as well put five or six slices of maple and honey smoked bacon on there while you are at it."

"No problem, son," she said with another big ole country grin on her face. "That's why you are growing up, getting so tall and handsome. I feeds my baby well. Look at those big shoulders and strong arms."

I smiled to myself. *She thinks I'm handsome! Yeah boi!*

"You are going to be one fine specimen of a man. Yes. My baby is handsome. Look at you, with your hair all wavy on the sides and those silky twists on the top. I love it. And look at that bright smile of yours. Your teeth are perfect! Yes Lord! My baby is good-looking and fine! Lord, have mercy! The world is in trouble now! I love your smile, son. A man's smile can take him far in this life. It shows he is kind and polite. It can buy you an audience with just about anyone. Always be kind to others, son. Let your God-given features be a gift to the world and use them for good."

"Man, Momma, why are you treating me like I am a baby! I know these things already! You've been saying them all my life! I hear you!" I turned, and looked at her to smile, but her back was already turned, and she was facing the stove, filling my order. "Wow! Momma thinks I'm handsome."

It was a meal fit for a king. She placed it before me with such care and love. She never served me on paper plates. She always used her best china for all of my meals. Even as a little boy, I remember eating from her best tableware, the special set she displays in the vitrine.

I didn't have to ask for extra warm syrup, whip cream, extra melted butter, fresh blueberries on the side, also warmed, and napkins. She had it all there like she always did. She laid her special bread knife on the table as

well, right next to my brass fork. She knew I didn't like cutting through my pancakes with my fork.

"Apple or orange, today son?"

"I'll take apple."

She smiled, went to the refrigerator, poured a huge glass of both orange and apple juice, brought them back to the table and gently placed them in front of me. As she shuffled back toward the refrigerator, she rubbed me on my shoulder warmly and smiled. She filled a second glass with only ice. She knows I like my juice extra cold to the last drop, so she always fills another glass with ice so that my juice does not become diluted as the ice melts. I whispered, "Thank you," but I said it so low because I didn't want her to hear me.

She began singing her favorite song as she shuffled around the kitchen, cleaning and putting the leftover food away.

Lord, don't move my mountain,
But give me the strength to climb,
And Lord, don't take away my stumbling blocks,
But lead me all around.

Her voice was so melodious and filled with so much passion and pain. Even the cracks were heartfelt. I loved hearing her sing... I sat there for a minute and closed my eyes. My heart felt as if it was being prepared for something noble whenever she sang. It drew me in like a faint light in a dark forest. The world around me was ever so dark, but Momma's righteous voice would always lead me to the light. *How did that come to be her favorite song?*

"There you go, singing that song again! Momma, what's up with you and that song? I'm tired of hearing you sing that song! There are a million songs out there, and you pick that one every single day. OMG, Momma! Avia! Sing something else, for God's sake, please! That song is killing me right now! I've been hearing it for 17, almost 18 years now. Give me a break! 'Lord, Don't Move My Mountain. Lord, Don't Move My Mountain,'" I mocked disdainfully.

"You don't have a mountain, Momma. Are you aware of that? You need to stop singing that song. It makes me wonder about you, Momma. Are you missing a few marbles up there in your noggin?

The song is redundant. Just like you singing it over and over is redundant! The Lord needs to give you the strength to take that rag off of your head. That's it. That rag is a mountain. See, look at it, on your head like a big ole mountain. What are you, Momma? Are you a lumberjack? You have a lumberjack hat on your head and that big old lumberjack dress. Hiding your big old lumberjack stomach. The Lord has answered that prayer, Momma, and then some." I looked at her and gave her a sideways grin because I knew I was getting to her. She hates my insolence. It really hurts her. So, I kept pushing her buttons.

"Oh, hush, child."

"Don't hush me, Avia. All of my guys talk about you. They don't like you. One of them was just on the phone saying he doesn't know how I deal with you. He said that you are repulsive. Do you hear me? That's what my friend thinks of you! He just told me a few minutes ago on the phone! He asked me why you don't wear your hair and why you shuffle around like an old lady. I told him I've been asking you that for years, and I still don't know the answer. So, why don't you wear your hair, Momma? Why do you shuffle around this house like some old rundown slave mammy? My friend said that dress you wear everyday stinks, too. He said you stink, Momma. Do you know how embarrassing that is? You stink, Avia. When is the last time you took a bath, old lady? You look like death. Do you have to smell like it too?" It was a lot of fun talking about that old grungy woman. Looking like an old bag lady.

"His mom wears high heels and looks good in them too, and she always wears her hair. She goes to the beauty shop and everything. You have nice hair, Momma. I've seen pictures of your hair when you were young. You wore lots of nice styles. I love the picture on your dresser in your bedroom, and all the ones in your picture albums. You look good in those pictures. You were a fox! What happened to you, Avia? For real, Momma, what's up? I will even pay to get your hair done. I like that short, sassy look on some of your pictures. It gives you that raw, bad-girl, Fantasia look, when she sang the song, 'If You Don't Want Me Then Don't Talk to Me.' You know what I'm sayin'? That's the Momma I want. If you do that, Momma, you can have these fools eating out of the palms of your hands... Walking around here looking like an old rusty jalopy is not the answer. You don't have to do that, Momma. I can't stand it when a female lets herself go. That's one of the worse things in the world that a man has to look at, Momma. All you have to do is start taking care of yourself. You can be a 10 on the charts. You will be like Cadillac Records in no time. Those pictures prove that you could have gotten any man you wanted back in the day. And he would have been a fool to leave you. You were gorgeous, Momma. Gorgeous. But then again, I don't know. Tell me what happened. Why did you stop caring? How did you sink so low? This is a shame!

"And what's wrong with your face? Were you in a lot of fights when you were growing up? It looks like you lost every one of them. Your face is just so sad, Avia. Are you in mourning? And look at all those scuff marks in your face. What are they, burns? Bleach? Is that why my dad really left you? Did he leave because of how you look? It looks like somebody put a fire out with your face, Momma. And look at that long skid mark, Avia. Did someone burn rubber on your face from your forehead all the way down to your chin? Looks like a train track. Why don't you become a conductor or work on an oil rig? Or, better yet, just die already. Have you thought about that? But you know what, it doesn't matter... IT DON'T MATTER, Avia, because females like you are asking for it. You are asking for these men out here to disrespect and check you. That's why I check these females. A female needs to be checked from time to time. I check them on the regular. You know what I mean - choke them up."

I got in her face and pretended my hands were claws as if I had them wrapped around a broad's throat and I started shaking them back and forth like us men have to do these chicks from time to time. "They learn quick when you choke them up, Momma."

I started laughing and waited for her response... She did not respond. "Do you need me to put my hands on you, Momma? I don't have a problem doing that. I'll hook you right up! Just ask me. Give me a reason. I think my powerful hands around your scrawny neck is the perfect fit. I'll have you gasping for air in no time. It will feel just like a necklace, or a necktie, a string of pearls, or one of those big rapper chains, or maybe even one of those ridiculous Flavor of Love Clocks."

Momma still didn't respond to me. She kept moving around, trying to get her work done and get out of my way. But I wouldn't let her. I dominated her easily. She was small and minuscule. She was insignificant. She was a nose wipe. Momma was nothing at all.

I followed her around the house, antagonizing her, mocking her and making fun of her. She was weak, and I despised her. I shuffled behind her like I was a crippled old hag, talking and mimicking her squeaky, mousy voice.

"Boy, Momma! This is a good day! Look at all the fun we're having! We are both old hags! How do you feel, girl?"

Momma wasn't feeling me today. She didn't say a word, but I was on a roll.

"Naw, naw. Here it is. I know what to do. Let me get you a man, Momma. BOOYAH! See! I told you I got you! I know plenty of guys out there that will have you, Momma. I know a few spots. Now, he may have a drinking problem, but judging from your looks, he needs to be drunk to look at that train wreck of a face, anyway. You know what I'm saying? And you got to learn how to respect a man, Momma. Drunk or not, can't no woman EVER disrespect a man. See, one thing y'all females got to remember is this... Y'ALL CAN'T BEAT US. We will knock y'all out. Point blank. Period."

"Aaron, get on out of here and go somewhere. Get on to school."

"See? See how mean you are, Momma?" I said, laughing. "You can't even take a joke. I'm your son, playing around with you, trying to have fun with my momma, giving you pointers on how to get a man, and you talk to me like that. You are so mean!"

"Hush your mouth, Aaron! Now hush! You don't know anything about men and women, but one day, you will learn. Now get on out of here, and take your disrespectful butt to school, and learn something other than this foolishness you are talking. I have raised you better than this!"

Taunting Momma was the only way I could pay her back for lying to me about my father. I don't care what she says; I know good and well that she did not have a one-night stand with my father.

"I'm not your little boy anymore, Avia. I don't believe anything that you say. I'm grown. I'm a grown man! I know a lie when I hear one, Avia. Tell me about my father, Avia! Why don't you speak about him? All you've ever said is that he moved away before I was born, and that you have not heard from him since. You moved around a lot, Avia. Why? Was he looking for me, and you kept moving around just so he couldn't find you and see me? Is that it?"

Avia had tears in her eyes, but I liked it when she cried. I made her cry a lot. I wanted to hurt her for being a liar. She shuffled slowly into the living room and sat down in her Lazy Boy, and mumbled in that broken, squeaky tone, "Shut your talking, Aaron! Just shut your talking, boy."

"I'm not going to shut my talking, Avia.
WHERE IS MY FATHER?!
WHAT IS HIS NAME?!
WHY WON'T YOU TELL ME ABOUT HIM?!"

"I said hush your talking."

"Listen to yourself, Avia. You sound stupid. Telling me to hush my talking is not an intelligent answer to my questions. I have said this to you a thousand times. How stupid are you, Avia? How many times do I need to teach you this lesson? This is why I mess with you! You are an unreasonable old lady. You do this stuff on purpose to get on my nerves! Man, Momma, I deserve to know what's up!

TELL ME ABOUT MY FATHER!

Avia clocked out on me. She didn't say another word. That means I am still the reigning champion of our family chats. I always win against that little thing. She can't out-talk or out-think me. She always walks away like a bird with two broken wings. I love that part of the game! I roasted her like a piglet. She was burnt to a crisp. My words were hot. I was on fire. I don't know why she continues to get in the ring with me. My nonstop belligerence and ongoing interrogations drain all the emotional wind out of her. But I suppose she doesn't challenge me too strongly because she knows what I will do to her if she does.

My work, for the moment, was done. And so was the devil's... He was finally done tampering around in my head, pushing those mischievous buttons. The pressure was lifting!

Man, I got to take a leak! But I love this game!

Teaching
MOM-
ENTS

"Lord, don't move my mountain," Momma sang quietly to herself.

"I feel 10 gallons lighter, Momma!" I'm ready for round two of our morning chat. Are you? If not, you better get ready! I'm geeked up and running on a full battery! Com' on, girl, let me make you a star. I'mma record our discussion and that face of yours live online. You will be famous after that... in a meme kind of way, of course." I cracked up laughing because I knew she did not have a clue about live streaming or memes!

Momma continued tuning me out. I could tell I had gotten to her because she closed her eyes, hesitated, and began singing again... "Give me the strength to climb..."

"Yeah, this video will make you strong, Momma. It will give you strength to throw that mountain out the window!" I took my phone out and started waving it around in her beat-up face, but still did not get a rise out of her. *Man, my aim is off!*

"Instead of singing, Momma, why don't you try fixing yourself up? That way, I can bring some of my friends around here without being put to shame by this clown act you are pulling."

"And Lord, don't take away my stumbling blocks..."

"I don't know what kind of deal you and The Lord have with this mountain... this imaginary mountain that you want strength to climb... I have news for you, Momma. Look around, Avia! Do you see any mountains in here? I don't think so! That mountain ain't coming. But what you can do is ask The Lord for strength to start walking up that hill at the end of the block. You need to exercise anyway! You are looking pretty frumpy, all out of shape, with that big old stomach... trying to hide it with those baggy dresses. That's the mountain, right there. Nobody wants to look at that, Avia, straight up! Talking about 'don't move my mountain!' Your face is the mountain, Avia. You must have upset the cosmos pretty bad to be born looking like that! How many more mountains must I tolerate! Your ugly face is my mountain! I don't deserve this foolishness, Avia! Why do you torment me like this?"

    "But lead me all around.

    Lord, I don't bother nobody.

    I try to treat everybody the same,

    but every time, I turn my back,

    They scandalize my name.

    But oh Jesus.

    You don't have to move my mountain

    But give me the strength to climb"

    "Whatever, Momma."

    "Aaron, finish up your breakfast, and get on out of here! You and all your foolish talking, making yourself late for school again."

    "You see, Momma. This is why I do you like I do. When I'm expressing myself to you, you sit there and tell me that I am a fool. That makes me furious. Always talking to me like I am a child. I'm a grown man. This is my house. Always holding secrets from me and not giving me the information I need to move around. Like I'm not smart enough to process the stuff YOU decide I don't need to know. You are getting me mad, Avia. You and all your lying ways."

"Aaron, hush. Calm down. I'm not trying to stir you up this morning. I'm just saying. At this rate, you are going to miss your entire first-period class. This is your senior year and you are doing so well. I am so proud of you, son. Don't risk it now. School will be out in just a few weeks."

"Momma, what did I tell you last year and the year before that? School is for suckas! Did you think I was talking just because I'm good with words? I know I talk a lot of stuff, but this is real. Listen to me. This is a teaching moment. I get more education doing what I'm doing right now. I'm an entrepreneur. Being in business for yourself is what's up."

"Oh yeah?"

"Yeah! You sound like you don't think I can do it? Are you saying I can't have my own business? I am good with computers, Momma. I can build game applications. I am good at that stuff. I can beat the system. I'm telling you."

"You can, huh? Are you sure that is what you are doing, though?"

AAAAAVIAAA! I SCREAMED AT THE TOP OF MY LUNGS! I saw Avia's face change. I love it when her face changes. I could feel my mouth watering. I could taste her fear.

I paused ever so slightly, swallowed the saliva secreting beneath my tongue, then jumped up from my chair in a rage, flipping the breakfast table upside down in the process, knowing that this would put more fear in that

weak thing. Pancakes, bacon, and special forks and knives shot in all directions of the kitchen. Orange and apple juice dripped from the ceiling and slide down the walls like rain.

"I'M GONNA KILL YOU, AVIA!" I said as I move toward her with both my fists clinched in a tight knot! "WHY DO YOU ALWAYS PUT ME DOWN? WHY?" She tried to shuffle away from me, but I could out pace that turtle shuffle any day – even in my sleep. Before she could take a few steps, I was already in front of her with a pancake in my hand that I had picked up from the floor.

"Where are you shuffling off to, old lady?!" Her eyes bucked wide open.

"ANSWER ME!" I yelled, while blocking her attempts to scoot around me. I pushed her backward. She stumbled but caught her balance. I shoved her harder and she fell to the floor."

"Look at you! You are good for nothing. You are just a weakling. Down there on the floor with the trash." I threw the pancake at her. It slapped her in her silly looking face before bouncing off and hitting the floor.

"What have I told you about messing up this house, AVIAAA!" Pick that mess up. PICK IT UP NOW, LIL' GIRL. PICK IT UP!"

I watched in sidesplitting stitches as she sat there on the floor trying to scrape all the food in a pile.

"That's right, that's a good doggie. Now you know what to do." I took my foot and put it against the pancake that pimp slapped that slapable face and shoved it even closer to her. She looked up at me with that broken, defeated look again.

"EAT IT! Come on, doggie. Eat it! Don't nobody care about you looking all stupid, Avia! You should have thought about that before you put me down. Who's down now, Avia! EAT IT!"

I wiped the sweat from my brow with my forearm, then raised my foot and smeared the soft, mushy pancake from the bottom of my gym shoe onto Avia's mouth. She turned away and I just laughed.

"You always did make a big mess when you eat.

"Now get up off the floor, looking like a mangy dog begging for scraps." I reached down and yanked her up from the floor with just one jank on her scrawny arm. It felt like it was going to plop right out of that dried up socket it was in. But man, why does this game become less fun every time I play it?

"Man Momma, look at you, always falling. What's wrong with you, girl? Do you need to be in a nursing home or something? You can't even stand up without falling. I'mma stop worrying about it though, because every few days I look around and there you are, back down there on the floor. But since you are a lowdown dirty dog anyway, the floor must feel like home."

***

I tore off a few paper towels from the roll. "Here, wipe off your face." I then brushed pancake off her smock. "You have food all over your clothes. Why are you so sloppy, Momma? You eat like an animal. What are you, a pig?" A life-sized grin plastered across my entire face. I couldn't stop laughing. Momma was a joke to me.

"It's alright son, I'm okay."

"I know you are. You're always okay. Slaves are built that way. They take everything ole massa do to them and still keep right on ticking. That's your best quality, Momma... that slave mentality. You belong in the "Big House, girl!" But enough of your aristocratic assets, what were we talking about before you messed yourself? And I mean you messed yourself. Look at you; it's a doozy this time... I don't hear you, Avia. I asked you a question..."

"We were talking about your accomplishments, Aaron."

"Ok, carry on, girl..."

"Your accomplishments are great, son. And I have no doubt that you can, and will, do great things."

I smiled and shook my head, "Yes... I will."

"And yes, you CAN beat the system! But no one beats these streets, baby. The street is not a gamble. It's a pending death trap, and that's not the route for you. You are smart, Aaron, talented and handsome. But you still need your education, baby."

"But you didn't finish school, Momma. Don't say nothing to me! You didn't go to college! You probably didn't even finish high school, did you? Always around here bragging about how smart you are. I'm smart too, Momma. You just act like you can't see it. But I don't need no education either. I have ways of making money!"

"Aaron baby, listen to me."

"No Momma, I'm serious. The truth of the matter is, no matter how mad you make me, I plan on taking care of you. I mean I can see that you have done alright. You have made a real nice home here. But I want more than this lil' ladida stuff. Compared to what I can do, this ain't nothing but chicken scratch. I want you to have more than chicken scratch, and I can't get it in no classroom. I don't need to sit up there listening to all those fake teachers lie to me, Momma. Most of them don't like me. Did you know that? And most of them don't look like me. I have already peeped them out. They don't teach real history. I know the truth. I read and do research. And check this out; did you know I still use my library card? Nooo! That's because you don't pay attention, Momma. Plus, I have a whole library of my own upstairs filled with authors I like: DuBois, Malcolm X, Booker T, James Baldwin, Frederick Douglass, Langston Hughes. Brothers like that, Momma. I even have some Toni Morrison and Gwendolyn Brooks up there. And listen, this one's by Claude McKay,

IF WE MUST DIE

If we must die, let it not be like hogs
Hunted and penned in an inglorious spot,
While round us bark the mad and hungry dogs,
Making their mock at our accursèd lot.
If we must die, O let us nobly die,
So that our precious blood may not be shed
In vain; then even the monsters we defy
Shall be constrained to honor us though dead!
O kinsmen! We must meet the common foe!
Though far outnumbered, let us show us brave,
And for their thousand blows, deal one death
blow!
What though before us lies the open grave?
Like men we'll face the murderous, cowardly pack,
Pressed to the wall, dying, but fighting back!

"You see, Momma. That's raw. Claude McKay killed it. And I'm doing exactly what he said in the poem... I'm fighting back. That alone is a victory. It's a victory that transcends my personal issues with this problem. It's a victory for the revolution of black souls, Momma... it's a win for black people.

"Listen, I know I'm always angry, but I have good reason. You moved me to this uppity neighborhood, Momma, with all these uppity black folks in it. Then you enrolled me into the school way across town. And I am sure you had good reason for it. But did you know that all the African American male employees at that school are janitors, lunchroom assistants or security guards? Did you know that Momma? There are only two black male teachers in that entire school, and one is a coach. I bet you didn't know that either. There are over 4,000 students at that school, and over 3,000 of them are African American. Half of the other 1,000 is Hispanic. And, the leftovers are Caucasian, Asian, and other. It's a real Mulatto mix in that joint. I'm not buying it. I make straight As, Momma. You know this, ALL honors classes. You know this. I can do that Simple Simon work that they assign us in my sleep. This, you also know. I have always been in the top one and two percentile of my class, but what did they do, Momma? They tried to dummy me down.

"Do you think they are considering me for valedictorian? Do you think they are going to select me to give the graduating class speech? Do you think I am going to be Salutatorian, Momma? I think not. I'm a threat to them, Momma. They fear me because I am educated. They hate me because I call them out on the whitewashed history, they try to smear all over our brains. I don't go for it, Momma. I'm not that vulnerable like that. I know real history. I come with the facts. And they hate me for that. They hate that I'm smarter than them and that I am not complicit with their divisive plans to program me. I've spoken to the principal and even many of the teachers. None of them responded favorably, Momma. Things are still the same."

"And don't get me wrong, Momma. I'm not against education and learning institutions. Not at all. But THAT school is for suckas. Lots of black men are educated and have degrees, teaching degrees, all over this urban city, Momma, and should be teaching black and brown students that look like me, right there at that run-down sham of a school. In my opinion, it hasn't earned the right to be called a learning institution because all they are trying to do is program us. That's why they still use that antiquated system and hire "Massa's children" and have them sweeping and mopping the floors, cleaning the toilets, and shooting a basketball in gym class, just to keep us in our place. They refuse to let the black teachers shine, Momma. They don't want us to see powerful men of color. Powerful men that look like me. They are afraid that we will discover our power, then rise in strength and influence. They are afraid that we will do to them what they have done to us! But, from all my research, the only movements we engage in are movements to fight for equality and unity, fairness and impartiality. Someone is painting our motives with a dirty paintbrush, Momma. And it ain't us!"

"I'm cool with every single one of the black staff members that work there. I've spoken to the black janitors and lunchroom helpers at one point or another. Some, I have developed good relationships with. Many of the black staff at that school went to college, Momma. Did you know that? But look where it got them: cleaning off tables in the cafeteria and pushing around mop buckets. Frankly, those black staff members care more about us kids than the teachers. They actually talk to us in the hallways and ask about our lives. They are the ones who need to be teaching us. I betcha we'll excel then. But they are too scared to fight for their rights or for us. They need to stop being cowards. That's all they are, a bunch of weak cowards!"

"Aaron, you are speaking too quickly, boy. You don't know anything that your young mouth is spewing. Watch your tongue, son, and how you put your mouth on others. I've taught you better than that. Now please son, listen to me. THIS IS A TEACHING MOMENT! You don't know their stories. All you know is what they told you. All those jobs are respectable jobs, performed by respectable men and women, taking care of their families. You should honor that. We don't look down on anyone that's doing what they have to do. And just so you will know, going to college did not get them where they are. RACISM and PRIVILEGE simply keeps them there."

"I hear you, Momma! And I'm not looking down on anyone. I'm looking down on the system. The system is not right! And I will never settle for Massa's scraps that he hands out to make me believe that he is a blessing to me. And I am not talking about those low-scale, menial jobs he set aside for us, Momma. I am referring to this huge, global issue of inequality designed to break us like change from a dollar. It props them up like insignias of honor. No disrespect to those who are, but I can't. I just can't."

"You just can't, hmmm? Momma said. "But you can be a drug dealer. Hmm, boy? That's what you call respectful and fighting the revolution, Aaron? Hmmm! What's respectable about that?!"

"Wait! What are you talking about, Momma? Drug dealer? I don't know where you are getting your information from, but I think you got me mixed up with your man, old lady."

"Now, don't go getting disrespectful. I'm just talking to you. Just don't play me for no fool. You are my son, Aaron, and I love you. It's dangerous in those streets, son. I want you to be safe. Being a young black man, you are not safe! Don't put yourself in harm's way. There's a bullet out there for every black man that is born. And like you say, that's FACTS, Aaron. I'm just talking to you, telling you the facts. You must be strategic if you want to have any chance of dodging the bullet that has your name on it, son. At the end of the day, all I want you to do is come home. Come home to me, son. Don't let them get you."

"Whatever, Momma. They won't even see me coming. They will look around and wonder when it started raining. Only it's not rain. I gets up early in the morning to handle my bidness. And, I'm telling you, Momma, it's nothing like that first leak of the day."

"Aaron, are you sure you are not going to the other side of town, hanging out, selling drugs, and doing God knows what else?"

I immediately thought about the work I put in last month. But ay, it's either get or get got. I walked around the mess Momma made in the kitchen and went to the stove and grabbed a few more of those pancakes and several slices of my maple and honey smoked bacon.

"Come on, Momma. Why do you always think the worst of me? I am not selling drugs or doing anything that will cause me to catch a case! Somebody is feeding you bad information. Who are you talking to? Do you even listen to me? I've already told you that I am working on my game applications. My friends are not just my friends. They are my business partners, Momma. We are forming a real corporation. Everything is shaping up. All the pieces are coming together just like I planned. You just wait and see. I'mma make you proud of me, Momma. That's if I don't kill you first!"

Momma rolled her eyes at me and shook her head in disappointment. I started laughing.

"Man, come on, Avia. You know how I do. Ease up and stop working your panties into a bunch! Let me have my fun!"

"Aaron, that's no way to address me, son."

"Avia please, it's a joke! Laugh a little! You act more like a bad teacher than a good mother. I just poured out my heart about how I am going to make you proud of me, and all you can focus on is some stupid joke. That's why I can't stand you, that right there. You haven't said a word about being proud of me!"

"I'm proud of you Aaron, but that's not the point. Your attitude is the point and may get a gun pointed in your face, baby. That's the point! That's the point I have been making your entire life. Be respectful in this world. Money isn't everything, baby. Success is more than a large bank account. I want to see you become all that you are destined to become. Character is like the gold card of credit, son. If it's good, it will open doors in your life that would otherwise be closed. You are so much bigger and smarter than this crooked system and these streets. Be a respectable man, baby. By all means, invest and build a legitimate game corporation. You can do that with your eyes closed. And it doesn't have to be 2:03 A.M. in the morning either!" I raise a brow and look at her sideways with a big grin on my face. "What do you know about 2:03 A.M. in the morning, Momma?"

"Momma knows game, too, baby. But I know more than just game. I know that there is something surer, and more real than those streets, honey. Develop as many game applications as you desire. That's awesome. But never forget what's important in life, Aaron. Your legacy is important. Who you are as a man is the most important thing that you leave behind in this world. The way you live is your legacy. Give in life what you want to be reproduced. That's living, Aaron. And all Momma wants is for you to live your best life."

"Ok Momma. But why do you have to be so mean about it?" Momma smiled.

"You know, when you were about five years old, we had a neighbor with a daughter around the same age as you. Her parents would let her come over and play

with you. This particular time, you both were sitting at
your little blue plastic table set looking at a book. It was
filled with lots of pictures. I remember you explaining to
her so patiently and so thoroughly what each picture
meant. You were so articulate at five years old. I knew
then that you were special. And just like you read to that
little girl, I read to you every night before you went to
sleep, and many times during the day. You used to love
our time together at the library. I did too, Aaron. I
introduced you to every author I could think of. That's
why you love DuBois, and Malcolm, and Booker T... I loved
them; and I instilled that same love and passion into you.
You can't help but read and love knowledge. It's in you,
baby. I am a major part of who you are. And you know
why I enrolled you into that school? Sure, I could have
enrolled you into the uppity schools right here in this
neighborhood. But I didn't. I had my reasons. Listen, son.
When I saw you reading to that little girl all those years
ago. I knew you had a charitable heart. I knew you would
grow up to be a compassionate, caring man. So, I began
nurturing that part of you. I exposed you to the blight of
people of color. I knew you would see the injustice in the
world and not stand for it; just as the authors you love did
not tolerate it. Righteousness is in you, Aaron. You are a
righteous young man. That's who you are. Never forget
that. I've always known that one day, this part of you
would rise up. Maybe some of those janitors and
lunchroom helpers need to see someone like you.
Someone who has a dream and courage. I believe you can
defy the odds, Aaron. No doubt about that. You are
already an anomaly. I see greatness in your future.

Nothing but greatness! And when you finally see it for yourself, give back. Give back strong. Reach back for those that do not have the vision that you have. Mentor some of these young men on how to be a good, successful black man – a man of character. Help them escape the street and the doom that is awaiting them. That would make me happy, Aaron. It really would."

"Slow motion, Momma. I don't know about all that mentoring others and thangs. But I feel you, girl. And I got you. But let me get out of here. I've got to go to "schooooool.""

"And stay out of trouble today," she said with a smile.

"Now, why do you want to change me, Momma? Trouble is my middle name."

Momma laughed. "Boy, get on out of here and go to school!"

"Ok, but one more thing, Momma."

"Yes. What is it child?"

"I meant to tell you... the real reason I stopped letting my friends come over is because they say you look like Respusia, from Norbit, the Eddie Murphy movie." I said laughingly.

"Really? You just had to mess it up. I was enjoying these last few moments with you. But then you say something crazy like that and just throw water all over it and ruin it. It's just not in you to do right, is it child? Can you end on a good note, just one time?"

"NOPE!"

"Whatever, child! Bye Aaron. I love you."

"Bye, Momma. I mean Respusia!"

About

THE
BUSINESS

"Gap! I'm outside! Come on! We got bidness. Let's go!"

"Ace! Stop yelling on my phone! Out!"

Gap moved slower than he normally moved when Aaron showed up late. He was irritated by his dad's new girlfriend. She ate the last two pieces of bacon. He fried six strips last night for his dinner and wrapped the last two strips in a piece of recycled aluminum foil which he tucked way in the back of the refrigerator behind the rotten head of lettuce on the bottom shelf.

She had both strips laid out on her plate like a couple of snakes courting the last two eggs in the house, which were scrambled with the last slice of cheese, alongside the end piece of sliced bread, also, which was a part of his morning breakfast plans.

Gap glanced over at the sofa and could tell by the bottle of aspirin turned on its side and multiple pills scattered all over the table, and the duo cups of coffee on the coffee table, that both she and his dad were recovering from hangovers and a night of partying and wasting money and time.

Gap huffed heavily, muttered a few choice expletives under his breath, then headed toward the front door.

47

"What you say, boy?! Speak up, with your nappy head! Ain't no mumbling in here today!" his father boomed. "This is my house, chump. Don't be disrespectful. Come over here and say good morning to your new momma. She will be staying here for a while. Or, at least until tonight!"

Her laughter was loud and round as Bundt cake. Her overly massive jowls crowned her fatuously grinning face like a prom queen's tiara.

Why does he always bring these broads home and introduce them to me as my "new momma?" Gap vacillated back and forth, from the center of her face to the outskirts of her jowls, trying to distinguish where it all ends and begins. All the grooves gave him the bubble guts. He smiled as he approached the sunken sofa.

Her eyes, nose and mouth blended seamlessly with her glowing jowls while disappearing in the immensely doughy layer of pinkishness. Amused at her tightly fitting sheathing of skin, accompanied by a beignet of audaciously unapologetic brown, black, and beige freckles, protruding moles, and more pink meat dangling loosely from both jowls and the underlayer of exposed chin, he sticks out his right hand and greets the mound of life-substance before him. "Pleased to meet you, Momma."

"That's right, boy. You know the routine! What you think of her, boy?" His dad turns toward the pinkish, brownish, blackish, whitish, beigeish, frecklish, moleish, meatish, danglingish, clump of last-night-ish... "See, what did I tell you last night, baby? The boy is crazy about you already. Now keep yo' eyes and hands to yourself, boy. This one's all mine."

The loud, round Bundt cake blast bellowed from her bacon, eggs, and end-bread filled stomach once more. Gap tried smiling, but his new mom was really hard to condone.

She was strange as a goblin shark, and just as pink. Her clammy, pink freckly face was ladened by a lavish amount of flyaway blond hair. Though greasy and somewhat matted, he could tell it could be quite beautiful when groomed.

She definitely rubbed him the wrong way, and not because of unrivaled, unforgettable, and unbeatable looks!

In his opinion, she was a lot easier on his stomach than some of his other mommas his dad dragged home. He didn't like her because she was eating his bacon, and the last two eggs, and the end piece of the bread. The end piece was his favorite piece. He was looking forward to toasting it in the same pan that he would have scrambled his eggs in. He liked it that way.

That is a selfish broad, he thought to himself. Who comes to someone's home and eats the last of their food? A selfish woman, that's who! She needs to go - just like a pair of breaks when worn down to the steel. He needs to get rid of this broad! She ain't my momma!

The laughter kept booming out of the small, circular opening punctured dead center in her massive face. Well, almost dead center. It was pushed over to the left just a smidge by the ambitious layers of blushing pink. Her laughter was one of those things that did not come with a mute button. There was no escaping it. It made a grand, show-stopping entrance every time, kicking down the tavern door and filibustering its way to the stage. There was simply no pumping the breaks on that ride.

After regrouping, he looked at his dad and sighed, "I gotta go, Dad. My ride's here."

"Whatever, say bye to your momma, boy."

***

Gap shut my car door like he was trying to pull it into the front seat with him!

50

"Bro! What's up? How many times I gotta tell you to stop abusing White Girl. You know this my woman, bro. She's special. You gotta be gentle with this broad. Show her some love. PUT SOME GAS IN HER TANK."

"Dude, you funny. But, my bad, bro. I had a rough start this morning."

"What? Your dad had you meet another one of his hoes today?"

"Yeah. But chill with the hoe jokes, bro. That's my momma you're talking about."

I looked at him, and we both cracked up laughing.

"Come on, Gap," let's go get this bread."

"Bet. Ay, stop up there at the McDonald's, let me grab a couple of them breakfast sandwiches."

"No need, bro." I passed him a plate wrapped in aluminum foil. "Special order from Avia's kitchen. Grits and all, bro." A huge smile slid across his face.

LATER THAT EVENING

"Bro! We killed it today," I said to Gap as we entered the house I purchased a few months ago through a private owner. It's a small home in a quiet neighborhood about 35 miles away from some of our major territory where our foot soldiers are. I chose a two-bedroom, with an attached garage, because I like the space. I have a little more room to work. Nothing fancy, but suits our needs. It's on a private corner lot with all the privacy we need to be discrete. The front and back yards are enclosed by lots of green shrubbery, leafy trees, and a tall privacy fence. I finished it off with a state-of-the-art security system.

"Man, Gap, this is one of our best days yet! And this is just what we took in from our foot soldiers. They are really stepping their game up, bro. We are looking at expanding again. These apps that I have been working on are a hit just like I knew they would be. Low visibility but high profibility."

"Ace, you wild, bro. Profibility? That ain't no word!" We both started laughing.

"Chill bro. It is a word. It's my word. I got it like that. I'm like Webster, or his son or something." We laughed again.

"But seriously, Gap. We are about to get into bed with the big boys now. We are getting much love and much respect. It's happening. You know how long we been putting all of this together. Now, the big dogs are watering at the mouth to give us a seat at the table. And that cool. All of them can eat. Just not for free. This ain't for the needy. This is for the greedy!" We laughed again. "Ace, stop, bro. You are killin' me. You are crazy, bro!"

"I know. But don't front. You are excited, too. But you know what else this means. It's not time for us to relax. We've got to watch our backs more than ever now. Double-crossers will be coming out of the woodwork, and haters will be coming for us left and right. Trust none, bro. They are smiling in our faces, but they bottom line is, they want what we got. And if we sleep, they will creep."

We unzipped our book bags, and three-hundred-seventy-eight thousand dead presidents fell onto the King size bed.

"You see, Gap. This is what I have been working for. Our territory is growing like wildfire. I told you to let

52

me handle things. I got respect out here, bro. We getting'
mad love, bro. They know to respect me... my soldiers,
these females, everybody. They don't want no heat."

"Yeah Ace. You wild, bro. They are showing you
mad love, bro. I respect that." I smiled and handed Gap
his regular cut plus an extra 20 Gs. Gap lit up!

"Thanks, bro!"

"Yup! I told you, bro. When I go up, you are going
up with me. But we still gotta be low-key... Keep staying
with your pops for now. It was a smart move when you
moved back home with him anyway. We don't want
unnecessary eyes on us. Keep living like you living, bro.
Don't change a thing. I have a few more loose ends I need
to put in place before we bust a move on these fools. We
don't want people wondering how you are living so lavish,
and the last taxable income you had was from working in
the lunchroom at my old high school, bro. You are doing
good. Just keep your head down. I have a plan."

"Man, Ace. I don't know how you young guns
come up with these masterminding schemes. It's genius,
bro."

"Well, that's it right there. I'm not your regular
youngsta. I'm cut from another piece of the cloth, bro.
The piece that was never connected to the other piece in
the first place. You know how I'm out there in them
streets. I ain't nothin' nice, bro. They look up and wonder
where all their good fortune is coming from. They say the
rain is good for business. I'm like, rain? But it ain't raining,
son. I'm facing the Mulberry Bush."

"Ace you wild, man. But that's what's up. You
earned your respect. All these computer apps you got

going, bro. I mean, everything is sweet. I'm just grateful you trusted an old head like me enough to cut in on your blessings."

"I got you, bro. When your mom left and took your brother with her, I knew I had to step in and be like a daddy to you. I didn't want you 'round here like no orphan or nothing.

"Shut up, Ace, you crazy, man. You younger than me, son! I got you by 6 years."

We both laugh. I picked up another stack of bills from the bed and tossed them to Gap.

Gap smiles, but doesn't hesitate stuffing it back into his book bag to add to his personal stash.

"Me and your brother were thick as thieves, bro. We started planning this back when I was a shorty in the 9th grade. When I found out that you and him were brothers, it was a rap. That's why, out of all those lunchroom workers and janitors, I chose you, bro. I had your back from that day to this. And besides, I liked how you treated him. I'll never forget that day you stopped by to see him. You had a pair of those new Jordan's for him. That blew my mind, bro. It told me that you were a nice guy, loyal. I peeped that about you right off the back, bro. It was just a matter of time before it came to this right here. I got you, bro."

"Thanks, bro. That's love."

"No prob. When your brother left, I knew you were the only replacement, bro. So, shut up, and let's get ready for tomorrow. We have that meeting to deal with this territory issue first thing tomorrow. We don't want them to see us coming. It's gotta be like, 2:03 in the morning."

"Yup, them fools won't see us coming. It trips me out how these fools be slippin'.

Gap and I went to the cellar to the hidden vault and put that cash with the rest of the rapidly mounting stash.

We got back in the car and drove to the location. We set everything up and then waited for them fools. We had been casing the place for weeks. We knew how they moved. We knew what time they made their drops, how many guns they would have, everything. We even knew the exact location they would park their glitzy cars. And that's how we would get them. All three of the drivers were predictable and dumb. I don't know how people think they will be in business and don't know how to run one. You gotta have eyes in the back of your head in this line of work, fool! How you gon' be predictable? Great for me, but bad for you, son!

Like a rerun, they all pulled up at the same time, just seconds apart. Trelli, the Mexican bulldog sat in the backseat with his cellphone upside his head, waiting for his driver to open his car door. They never open the door of Trelli's vehicle until the other two cars took position. They were very strategic. One car in front and the other behind. They sandwiched Trelli's car as a sign of protection and importance. For us, it just made him a sitting Mexican. Both the first and last cars and all their passengers were blown to taco meat before their greedy, greasy fingertips wrapped around the door handle one final time.

Trelli turned white as a ghost when he finally saw me standing just a few inches away.

"Easy big fella. Easy. Hands up. Now slow, slow. That's a good dog. Both of you, go real easy and throw out your heat. Toss them into the bushes. Now, Gap, walk him around here.

Gap dug the gun deeper into his back. "Now move around, HOMIE." Gap said.

"And just so you know, Trelli. I don't have a problem killing a Rottweiler. Tell him Gap. He better recognize."

"Yup. His fingers are trigger happy, my mans. You better listen up carefully and do everything he says."

Trelli rolls his eyes. Ace smiles. Gap laughs.

"Make no mistake, pendejo, a mut like you, I have no problems with shooting right between those beady eyes you rolling, and watching you bleed out, it's just not fun..., it's necessary, but not fun." Ace said.

Gap laughs again. "You wild, Ace."

I laugh also. "How did you convince your Mexican mut brain, and all these Mexican mut brain fools with you, Trelli, that I was going to let you get away with disrespecting me by trying to sell your products on my corners, puta? You did not have my permission; and you did not pay tax."

"But it's not your corner, blood. It's nowhere near any of your neighborhoods where you do business, blood."

"Gap, do you hear this fool, standing here, looking me in all my African kingliness trying to educate me about the business, MY BUSINESS. What homie, you calling me a liar, you trying to educate me? Well, let me educate YOU. It is my territory. Why, because I said so. You don't run nothing up in these streets, you pendejo puta. And Gap, tell me, when did muts learn how to talk. Yeah, you definitely have mut for brains, you Mexican mut brain mut."

"Why are you doing this, homes? We have not disrespected you."

"Stop talkin', fool. Muts don't speak. They take orders, then wait for a treat to be tossed at them. Trelli, come on, man. Why does anybody do anything? The same reason why you tried to steal territory from me. It doesn't matter that I did not claim it at the time you disrespected me. You knew that I would claim it. You know that's the game, man. You heard the saying, "Wake a sleeping dog, and you his next meal, puta. Ain't no beating me to the punch, pendejo. So, that's why I am doing it, nigga. Because I can."

At that point, the driver elbowed Gap and tried to snatch the gun out of Gap's hand. It fell to the ground and slid a few feet away from them. The driver did a quick dive trying to get to the gun. I stood there in amusement. But I didn't do anything. Gap had to learn. And this was good a time as any to see what Gap had in 'em... I looked at Trelli and said, "See, this is why you don't deserve to be serving in my neighborhood. I've been good to you, Trelli, and this is how you pay me back. You come up here in my territory, park on my property, and then attack my guy. That's the thanks you give me for all the generosity I've shown you, Trelli?" Trelli didn't say a word.

"Gap! You bet not let this soft punk shoot you. Get up off that ground and beat all the taco meat out of that fool!"

Gap started growling and going wild. I laughed so hard. That mess was funny. But then, all of a sudden...

POW! POW! POW!

The shots came quick and close range, I couldn't tell if it was the gringo's blood or Gap's blood.

"That's what I am talking about!" I said as a bloody, out of breath Gap stood to his feet as the victor and reigning champion of our latest turf squabble.

Gap raised both his trembling hands in the air, looked down at the dead clump of Mexican on the ground. Kicked him, then kicked him again.

"See Gap, that's what I am talking about. I'm glad you all came to an agreement. I knew you could get him to see things our way. That's what's up." Gap was still standing there shaking with his hands trembling in the air and blood dripping from both his elbows. "Put your hands down, Gap. You did good." I stood there for a second to make sure he was okay. His hands began to slowly steady and stop shaking. And within moments, they were back at his side. But I could still see that ever-so-slight twitch still vibrating in his trigger finger. "Bro, you okay? Relax your hand. Chill. It's over. You are still the reigning champion." Gap could barely smile back at me. He nodded slightly before turning to Trellis.

"And as for you, we were going to let you live, greedy gringo trash. But look at you now. How does it feel to eat a bullet?" Gap said as he unknowingly raised his hands back into the soft morning air.

Ace looked at Trelli. "Here's the deal. You work for me now. I own you. And all your territory is mine. But, I'm a fair man. You work it for me and all I want is 40%. That 40% buys you peace and your life. Try to short change me or double-cross me, and this is what you have coming."

Trelli held a look of indifference on his face.

"Gap, open the trunk." Trelli's baby Momma was tied up and gagged. Trelli looked at Gap with fire in his eyes as Gap pulled her out of the trunk.

"Now, here's the deal, Trelli. We've taken care of your entire team. Everyone you trust and depend upon is right here on this ground. This was your right-hand man. His blood is on your hands, Trelli. You did this. Try to double cross me again. Next time it will be your Momma, your baby momma, and your bastard gringo son. As you can see, we can get you and everything you love anytime we want."

Gap pulled her close and smiled while looking at Trelli with a taunting smile on his face.

"So, I already have a crew in place to work with you, Trelli. I'm generous like that. I wouldn't leave you out here on your own, man. Especially not with all the new responsibilities that come along with your new position. I have my own mans in charge, but you will work closely with him just like you did with your mans stretched out down there on the ground. He was a weak link if you ask me. He wasn't aggressive enough. He was lazy. But now it's up to you to step up. I want the product out there. I want you to double the profitability." Gap looked at me and started laughing.

"Give me your phone...."

"What's the password..."

"Gap hook this baby up to the scrambler..."

"And turn off his location."

"You will get your customers to trust my mans just as they trusted you. We have both your lives and secrets in the palm of our hands."

Gap reached in his pocket and pulled out Trelli's girlfriend's phone and waved in the air.

"The slightest inkling of disloyalty and distrust we feel, your entire family dies. And you get to watch. Feel me?" Then Gap showed him the video. It was a video of Trelli killing a kid. A kid that just happened to be the hothead wannbe thug teenage son of a beat cop's wife's best friend." Trelli dropped his head in disbelief when he saw the footage.

"Yeah, that's right. I got eyes everywhere fool. Somebody in your crew who you thought you could trust sold you out for a few bean burritos, homes... That's right, I got you by your Taco sauce meatballs, you greasy wetback, white boy, Mexican. How you gone try to be in good with Mexico, fool, and you in America? How in the Taco Truck did you get in deep with the Mexicans anyway? Mexicans don't trust White Trash like yourself? What's up, white boi? Naaah, forget about it. It don't matter right now. Gap, give him his girl. And oh, yeah. Give 'em both their new phones..."

Gap reached into his pocket and pulled out a pocket knife and cut the zip ties from her hands and ankles.

"Now, as a reminder… we have copies of this video of you carving up this young man. If anything happens to me, or anybody in my crew, the DA, the newspaper, and that grieving beat cop get the first copies. And you go straight to jail, for life. But enough of that. Let's get to work.

I PLEAD THE **5** TH

candid

conversations

"So Gap, tell me, bro. What really happened with your mom and dad?"

"Nothing, bro. It's like I've always said, my dad was a cheat, just like he is now. He used to drink, waste all the money and come home and beat on her. She got tired and left three years ago. End of story.

"Yeah, I get that. And I am sorry that she had to go through that. But what about you? Why did she leave you behind?"

"It's complicated. But I'm a whole grown man, bro. I'm not running behind my mom like a snotty nose child. That's dead. My mom was young when all of this started. She hooked up with my dad when she was only 12 years old. She was 13 when she had me. By the time I was eight years old, I realized that she could not handle being a mom or a responsible adult. My dad is 18 years older than her. He had no business even looking at her like that, but it is what it is now. Too late to do anything about it. But my mom lied to him about her age. She told him she was 16. You've seen my mom, bro. She looked 16, and older, even back then. But that stuff doesn't matter now. That's the past. All of us have invisible scars that we walk around with every day. That's just how life goes."

"Invisible scars... That's deep, Gap. What are you talking about... invisible scars?" I looked down at both my hands and flipped them up and down. "See man - nothing, no scars anywhere."

Nah, man. Listen to me. I'm here, my dad's here, and my mom is gone. That's a scar. I tried my best to step up and be the man of the house, you know, do the things that my dad didn't do. That's a scar, get it? He was older and was doing his best to keep up with her, and couldn't. Scar. My mom was young and wild. Scar. He also has that bad liver but can't stop drinking, bro. Scar. He pours it down his throat like he's drinking bottled water or Gatorade or something. Scar. I don't know how long he will be here. Scar, man. That's a scar. He might be checking out soon, too. He's living like he is ready to die. SCAR, GET IT?

"Yeah, I do."

"My dad doesn't work or anything anymore. There was a time he'd hold down a job, but most times, he didn't stay on them very long. Now that he's on social security and collects that check, he doesn't work at all.

"But back in the day, before I was grown, when I was a lil' shorty, I got a paper route and gave all the money to my mom. I would collect cans, cut grass, rake leaves, and shovel snow. But it wasn't enough. I even quit school and started working at McDonalds and some of the other restaurants as a dish washer and busboy. But she still left, bro. I guess I could have gone with her, but yo' boi wasn't feeling it, bro. I was fed up. Nothing I did was ever enough for my mom. I didn't think I could live up to the responsibility of taking care of her and my little brother. Man, I miss that lil' hothead. And these are my scars, bro."

"I feel you, bro. I miss him, too. But your mom is gone. She doesn't call and check on you. What's up with that?"

"I don't trip on that, bro. My mom is out there in them streets. She is on this same stuff we out here slinging. I think that has a lot to do with my dad being the way he is. Not that it's her fault that he checked out. Because honestly, he was gone way before they met. He was older and was doing his best to keep up with her and couldn't. The issue with them was he didn't know how to help her or tame her. And instead of reaching out, he checked out and just gave up."

"Bro, that's too bad. I'm sorry to hear that. But what about your little brother? I miss Bluff! Just talking about him makes me miss him more. I can hear him calling me right now...

"Aaaeee, Ace, Negroid! Whataup, block mon! Not black man, he called me block mon! That was his Jamaican accent. Just horrible! He'd have his cell phone in his hand talking to somebody, anybody... see me walking toward the car and stop talking on the spot. He would pull the phone away from his ear, let the window down, stick his arm out the window and then start yelling out the window. He was always glad to see me, bro. He lit up every time. Man, I tell you, he was my guy. I miss him. I haven't heard from him in a minute, though. But he's a real friend. And dude is smart like the internet. He is like a junior Einstein or J.C.R. Licklider, bro. And nobody, I mean nobody, can do math like him. He is a walking calculator! I used to test him, too, bro. I would say some crazy number like, "What's 6,543,879 times a gazillion?" He'd know the answer, bro. I'm telling you. I should change his name to percent sign! Smart joker!"

"That's true, Ace. He is definitely smart, bro, just like you. That's why y'all hooked up so easily. It's like y'all was a married couple or something!"

65

"Yeah, right, man. Chill out with that, bro. You dug too deep with that one, bruh!"

"Whatever bro, I'm just messing with you. But for real, y'all is the two realest people I know, man. Listen to me. It's like y'all are built for this game. Y'all have the brains for it. I can't come up with all this. I'm 24 years old, and can't begin to put thangs together the way you and that lil' snot nose boy did. I was envious of lil' man, too, with his short butt. I used to walk by his room and just stand at the door and listen to you and him putting it all together. I'm proud of you, bro. But that lil' dude had it. Before he left with my mom, he told me that he had to go to look out for her. He's cool, though. He's handling bidness. He was more worried about me than himself. He was trying to make sure I would be ok. But I got you, now, Ace, so, I'm straight. And don't worry about lil' bro, man. He will get in touch when he's ready. I know it. I just never thought I would be a part of something this sweet. You two lil' negros pulled it off."

"Thanks, bro. And yeah, you right. I got you. I got you, bro. And you're right about Bluff. That lil' dude is alright. I remember when I met him. He was coming out of the liquor store down there in Bello Heights."

"Bello Heights? What you know about Bello Heights?"

"I'm all about the bidness, bruh! But don't worry about all that! And like I was saying, Bluff was laughing at the old men standing around on the corner just past the liquor store, telling stories about their lives. As I was walking by, he spoke and said, 'Hey, these old cats is crazy, bro. They tell these wild stories from their past, and

I believe em' because you can't make this stuff up. If you got time, listen up, bro. They love a new face in the crowd.'

"I slowed down... he turned his bottle up, then passed it to me. I took a smooth gulp then passed it back. A couple hours passed, and we were still out there laughing, talking, sitting on old raggedy chairs and running in and out of the liquor store. And before I knew it, that was our spot. Me and Bluff became thick as thieves. As a matter of fact, we became thieves. We rarely bought anything from them judgmental people. We went in there to buy our liquor, and they came at us on that *Don't Be A Menace To South Central*, type stuff. So, from that day forward, we had to get them. And you know me, I don't mind changing the weather on a fool. I rain down on them like it's 2:03 on the dot.

"The only thing we purchased from them was maybe a pack of gum, or a bag of chips, bro, but every now and again, I felt generous and blessed them, though. I did that to keep the heat off and the suspicion down. They watched our every move, but could never catch us. It was wild. I enjoyed getting them, too, because they came at us wrong. We were regular paying customers, but they let us know what was up from jump. And they didn't try to play it off, either. Coming through the door, they let us know that they didn't want our money or our patronage. You feel me, bro? I was the right, wrong one, bro. They had to pay for that discriminatory, judgmental, stereotypical malarky. They had to pay for it every time we got thirsty. I rained on them fools like sprinklers. We walked out heavy whenever we marched up in that joint.

We walked up in there like we had cased a bank. We always got our drink on for free!"

"You and lil' bro ain't nothing nice!"

"Got that right!" I said, laughing. "But that's how we started kickin' it, and we've been kickin' it ever since, till bro left."

"That's love, bro," Gap said."

"Yeah, bro. And no matter where he is in the world, he will always be my Day 1. I got him, no matter what."

"Yeah, that's love."

"Yeah. He gave me a ride home that first day he met me, and the rest is history. We found out that we had a lot in common."

"Like what?"

"Like weed, you non-white, non-mulatto, all crude, ashy African American!

Gap almost died laughing. "Man Ace. You have lost your mind. You are a funny dude."

"Yeah! Since you got to know erethang! Weed fool. We had that ganja in common!"

Both Gap and I started laughing.

"Yeah, Gap, I stood around listening. Lil' shorty was right. Those old cats have some stories out of this world. I don't believe any of it, though, but Bluff would swear up and down that every story they told was real. They got in his head because he wanted to be on that gangsta stuff they were talking. They were nothing more than a bunch of old drunk men with no women and nothing better to do than sit around trying to impress each other with their woulda, coulda, shouldas... But it's definitely entertaining."

"Well, I don't know if what they say is not true. Because that's how Bluff is. He can sense things. Look how he knew you were a good dude. Fools be passing by that spot all day and night. But he stopped you and invited you into his circle. That's what I mean when I say he is smart. He stopped you for a reason, just like he let all those other cats keep moving."

"Yeah, he knew he would be leaving and wanted me to look out for your old behind! What are you, like 500, bro!"

"No! But I'm old enough to be yo' daddy, bro. Respeck yo' elders, son!

"Ooooh! Good one, bro!"

We both laugh.

"But seriously, bro. I am glad you are here, Ace. But enough about that. What's your story, bro? You talk to your mom like she's one of these clucks out here, like my mom. I don't think she deserves that, Ace."

"Bro, I keep telling you that you don't know my mom's like you think you do. She really do be buggin'. She's not in touch with reality."

"Gon' somewhere with that, Ace. Is she schizophrenic or something?"

"Nah, but she doesn't want to deal with reality, bro, straight up. Do you know she still thinks I am in school? High school dude! She was telling me just this morning that I better not miss first period. I'm like, whaaattt? I haven't gone to school since 10th grade. She doesn't know that I graduated early, bro. I finished all that

kindergarten, high school stuff with my eyes closed two years ago. I signed all the paperwork myself to graduate early and everything. She still doesn't know."

Gap shook his head. "Wow, bro, that's deep."

"Yeah, bro. Something is seriously wrong with her head. My mom had me at a young age, too. She was like 15 or 16 years old. She claims it was with some dude, a one-night stand."

"Wow! Really?"

"Come on, bro. My mom – a one-night stand? I'm not going, bro. She ain't NEVER like that. I have never seen a busta up in the crib. Neverrr! I'll knock that fool out if he did try. She KNOW I don't play that."

"Calm down, my brother. You are getting all worked up like you are about to put in some work right now!" Gap said while laughing.

"Forget that, bro. I can't believe nothing that comes out of my mom's mouth. All she do is lie. She is a liar, bro. I don't know why she keeps my father from me. But she shouldn't take that out on me. Like I told her, every black male needs his father. Now, I'm a whole grown man, and she is still holding out on me. Even on my birth certificate, she listed the father as unknown. What kind of crazy is that, bro? I told you that she is a psycho. That's why I don't have love for her like that. I don't trust her."

PHONE RINGS

"Gap, hold on, bro, let me take this..."

Gap nods.

"Ma, what's up?" I lowered my voice and turned my head toward the window because I didn't want Gap know it was my mom.

"I don't know what's up, Aaron. You tell me, baby. A very bad feeling just came over me, and now I am worried about you. I was asleep in my Lazy Boy when I woke up feeling eerie. I dreamed that you were shot and killed in the streets like a dead dog on the ground. I'm worried about you, son. I don't want anything to happen to you out there in the street. You are my only love. I can't go on if anything happens to you. I love you, baby. Come home, son. You have a good home and a warm bed to sleep in. Why are you out there like you are a motherless child or something? Come home, baby."

I glanced over at Gap but didn't say a word… He sittin' up there looking at me smirking with that funny grin on his funny looking face. I turned back around in embarrassment because he knew it was my mom.

"Okay, Momma," I whispered again. "I got you, girl. Talk to you." Then I hung up.

I looked back at Gap and put a half phony smile on my face and said, "These hoes out here be on a guy, right?" Then I hunched my shoulders. Gap laughed.

"Stop front'n bro. That wasn't no hoe. You was over there talking to your mom's. Trying to whisper. Fool I heard you! Your mom deserves a medal, bro. A whole medal for lovin' your spoiled butt."

"She trippin', man. Gap, you just don't know. She is treating me like I'm still a lil' boy. Talking about, "Where are you, Aaron? Why aren't you home? It's past your curfew." We started laughing; but then Gap lit right back into me.

"Bro... your mom is the bomb! She loves you to pieces. Straight up! Have you ever considered that she is telling you the truth about your pops?"

"NOPE!"

"Or... OR... that she has a good reason for not telling you the details about her relationship with your dad?"

"NOPE!"

"And... I think it is past time for you to accept that all this other stuff is just in your own imagination. It doesn't add up! Your moms ain't got nothing but love in her heart for you."

"NOPE!!! WRONG AGAIN! I'm not going. Her grits and eggs got you all tangled up in yo' head, bro. She keeps telling me that she got pregnant and never saw the guy again. LYING! She claims she never even knew his name! My mom ain't no hoe. She don't get down like that. She not gone' get with no dude like that, bro. You see my mom's bro. SHE AIN'T NO HOE OUT HERE LIKE SOME OF THESE HOES, BRO! And I'm supposed to believe that's how she got pregnant with me. That I'm some one-night stand mistake. That's a lie, bro. THAT'S A LIE! Why she doing this to me? She keeps telling me that after she got pregnant, she moved around for a while, and then once she had me, she settled down in this place. And we been living out here in this area ever since. But forget that. I don't buy none of that crap she spittin'. My mom's a liar. Every time her lips move, a lie push through them joint's, bro. Skip all that. She's from up north. I know her! Tell me, how is she going to have sex with a dude that she don't even know, get pregnant, then move to a whole nother state, and don't even let that fool know?! Nah. I'm not buying it. This one-night-stand mess is a bunch of crap. Straight up!" Now she calling me trying to spook me. Like something is about to happen to me. Man, I got some heat for these fools out here.

"Bro, stop always thinking the worst about your moms. Give her the benefit of the doubt! She's doing right by you. She is right there taking good care of you, bro... cooking, cleaning, washing your foul draws... come on bro, IRONING your clothes, waking you up so you don't be late for "school!"

"School. Ha ha. You got jokes. Real funny!"

"But I'm serious, Ace. She even feeds your crusty butt with brass forks and a special bread and butter knife! Who does all that unless they really care! Bro!!!! She deserves some respect."

"I feel you, bro. But still, she needs to stop all this lying. But you right... she does look out for your boi. I'll give her that. Now, come on, we been down here in the basement conversatin' for a minute. This is the third time this week we have cashed in at an all-time highBut we gots to be out if we want to repeat tomorrow. We have another heavy day and some serious moves to make...Time out for all this brotherly love, bonding type, conversation. Got ya boi all misty-eyed."

A Time
FOR GIFTS

"Avia, where are you, girl… Momma?" I yelled the minute I stepped through the front door.

She didn't answer. My heart began to pound. Where could she be? "Momma! MOMMAAAAAA!" I roared as I proceeded to move toward her bedroom, thinking she was taking a midday nap. Before I could take three steps, I heard her tiny feet shuffling toward the front of the house. She looked up and saw me, then looked at the clock on the wall.

"Aaron." She said with a smile on her face. "You are home early, son… Why are you home so early, baby? Shouldn't you still be in school?"

"Not today, Momma. We had a half-day today, but look around. Do you notice anything different?" She looked me up and down, top to bottom, from the top of my head to the bottom of my Jordans.

"Spin around until I tell you to stop."

I laughed but spun around and around like she asked me to do. "I don't know what this has to do with you answering my question, but whatever you say, Momma."

"Go faster!" She said with such excitement in her high-pitched, squeaky voice.

"When are you going to tell me to stop? I'm getting dizzy. You are trying to make me pass out, ain't you, Momma? I knew you were a slick lil' thang."

Her eyes light up more. She was so happy and having so much fun! "You can stop spinning. Let me look at you now. Nope, still don't. I still don't see anything different. You are the same old handsome boy I gave birth to almost 18 years ago."

"Not me, Momma. What do you see different in the house? Look over there on top of the TV." She looked at me and laughed.

"Boy, I saw you carrying that big gift-wrapped box in here from the laundry room window. Why do you think I came out of the laundry so quickly?"

"I don't know. I thought maybe you heard me calling you."

"Nope! I came to see my baby! I was trying to make it here to open the door for you since you were carrying that large box."

"What? You don't know what today is?"

"It's Thursday. Boy, the days keep rolling around so fast these days. Seems like yesterday it was Sunday."

"Yup, that's right, Momma, it's Thursday. But can you guess what else today is?"

"Nope, just tell me."

"Momma, how can you forget. It's my birthday. April, 1st. You never forget."

"Well, doesn't seem like I had to remember, seeing you bought yourself that big handsome gift. You could barely balance that thing on your arm without dropping it."

"Incorrect. But you are right on one part. I did buy a gift. The big box is just a flat-screen TV. I'm going to use my other one to test out my applications and games on. But what you probably did not see is the other box that was sitting on top of the box with the TV in it. That is the gift, Momma, and it is not for me. I bought it for you!"

"What... you purchased a gift for me, son? Bend down, and let me feel your head. Are you alright? Are you sick? Are you running a fever? Did you cut your toe and an infection has set in?"

"Stop Momma. I know it's my birthday, and I haven't been the best that I can be. But I got you something to make up for it. Open it up."

"Ok, but go over there in that closet and look on the shelf first."

It was a small, hand-sized box.

"Momma, what is this?" I said smiling.

"Open it, son. Happy birthday."

I tore the box open. It was a double-sided black and brown leather belt. Quite fashionable and expensive, if I say so myself.

"Momma, this is raw. Thank you!"

"You are welcome, son!"

"How did you find a belt with my name on it?"

"I didn't find it. You can't find a belt like this in the stores, child. This belt is special. It's custom-made. Just like you! You are some kind of special, son. And watch this." She shuffled toward me and proceeded to take the belt from my hands.

I gripped it a little tighter and started laughing. "No way, Momma. You can't take this back. This is the best gift I have ever had."

She laughed again. For the first time in my life, I saw my Momma, smile. I mean, really smile. The entire room lit up. I walked to the refrigerator to get a glass of water so she would not see me getting all misty-eyed. She shuffled right behind me with the belt in tow.

"See, look at this Aaron." She flipped the buckle over.

"See, I had your name engraved in it. The writing is a little small, and I left my glasses back there in the laundry room. Read it to me, child. Read it out loud."

"It says, Aaron, Momma."

"Ok, what else does it say. All that money I spent, it better have more than just your name on it." Tell me why her squeaky laugh seemed to be the most precious sound I had ever heard before.

"Ok, it says, 'Aaron is a Hebrew word meaning, High Mountain, Mountain of Strength, Exalted, Enlightened, and Bearer of Martyrs.'"

We both stood there quietly, taking it all in. Not the meaning of my name, but the moment we were in. That was a new place. I had never been there before. I wasn't sure what was going on between us, but I could feel some kind of veil or scar, or something being removed from between us. I could feel myself softening for her....

Maybe Gap was right. Maybe there was something invisible that was causing all this bad blood between us.

"Yes honey, I had nine months to decide upon a name for you. I did extensive research. Aaron was the only choice. There were a lot of good names out there to select from, but when I saw this one, I didn't look any further. I knew I was carrying a beautiful man-child, and something told me your name was Aaron."

"Look at you, Momma. This is great stuff, girl. Are you trying to make me hug you or something?"

She tried to shuffle and get away from me when I reached out to hug her, but I grabbed her and put both my arms around her.

"I'm sorry, Momma."

"It's ok, child. You know, I had lots of conversations with you when you were still just a poppy seed in my womb. Not a day went by that I did not remind you of how special you are and how great you are. I knew that you would be met with great challenges in life but, I also knew that you would conquer them all. And here you are, coming into your own. I think that you are ready to meet the world. I have every confidence that you will make wise and right choices. I love you, Aaron. I always will.

RING RING RING

"Momma, I've got to take this call. It's Gap. He's trying to celebrate with me. He's got this lil' party thang planned for me tonight that's supposed to be a surprise. But you know your son, Momma. Gap is not as smooth as your baby boy. I've been knowing about his "surprise" for the last two weeks."

"Hush, boy. You are a mess. Go on and be with your friends. This is enough celebrating for me. You've made my heart glad, Aaron. You've made your Momma's heart glad."

***

"Gap! What's up, bro. Where you at?"

"You know me, bro. I'm out chea!"

"You crazy, bro, you wild. I'm on my way to your crib now."

"Nah, bro. I'm not home. I'm at my girl's spot, over on One Lane. She's in the same apartment you came to the last time. She went out, don't know when she'll be back. Just pull around to the back, bro."

"Cool. Out."

Because of traffic, it took me about an hour to get there. It's usually a 20-minute drive, but there was a car accident, and the wreckage was still being cleared out. Once I made it to One Lane, I was shocked when I did not see a line of familiar cars in the back. Where is Jaxx's 1988 Classic Pontiac Bonneville SSE and JuJu's 1992 Saab 900 Turbo Convertible? These guys should be here. Where are my homies? Where is my party?"

I WANT MY BIRTHDAY CAKE!

"Gap, I'm out here, bro. Let's go."

Gap got into the car like it was nothing. He had on a pair of yellow Beats and appeared to be dancing to some old-school slow jams. He seemed delirious and off beat.

"Man, what's up? And what is you listening to, with them loud yellow Beats on, bro? All that bumping and grinding with the air... Where's your girl?"

"Man, she left. She gave me a headache, too. She took off about 3 hours ago, and I have not heard from or seen her. She's trippin'. Talking about she is tired of all my lies. Bro! What is she talking about?! What lies? That girl is in that voodoo, witchcraft, I-will-cut-a-cheating-man's-balls-off mess. I don't fool around on her, and she knows this, bro. I'm scared of her. She will kill me for real. You know this. She left out of the house talking about I messed over the wrong one, and I'mma get mine. I think she put some of that weird Louisiana, down in the Bayou crap on me. She took her underwear off, man, and rubbed them in my face before she left. Talking about I'm dead to her. What does her draws have to do with me being dead? She is trying to get in my head. She does that voodoo. She is plotting to do something to me, bro. She is going to hurt me, I know it."

"Straight up, bro?"

"Yeah, bro. And I don't know what she is talking about. I been keeping my head down, bro, and, you know me, bro. I don't fool around on my girl. Where is all this coming from? I'll tell you. It's coming from inside her sick head. She just likes messing with me. She's crazy, bro. Jealous for no reason. She already knows that if I ain't out here with you making this paper, I'm at home or with her.

She is accusing me of stuff I don't do. Fooling around with these other chicks out here, bro... For what?! That don't come to no good end. That can mess up our business, bro. So, I don't do it."

"Broooo!" I said laughing. "This girl's got you buggin'! But you right, though. She is just trying to get in your head. Don't let her, bro." I started laughing again.

"Why you laughing at me, bro? I'm hurtin' right now. I wouldn't laugh at you and none of these crazy girls you mess with."

Laughing hysterically! "First of all, bro, I would neverrrr be in this situation. How did you let this broad get in your head like this? Come on, bro. Really?" I held my hand out. "Come on bro, give it up - right now, give it up."

"Give what up?"

"YOUR PLAYA' CARD, BRO. YOU SPRUNG!"

We both cracked up on that one.

"Wow, bro, you right. So, what do I do, bro?"

"I don't know. That's your crazy, woman!"

"See, I told you she's crazy! You know it, too!"

LAUGHING HYSTERICALLY AGAIN!

"Come on bro, I'm just playin' with you, bro. Calm down. And stop stressing over this girl. That girl is crazy, straight up. But she is crazy about you, too. Y'all been together like forever. Y'all can sing with Heatwave, 'Always and Forever.' That's how long y'all been together."

"You funny, bro. Real funny."

LAUGHING AGAIN.

"Come on, bro, lighten up. I'm just messing with you. You need to get your mind off of this. Let's do something. Where do you want to go, bro? I got you."

"Let's go to the mall. Let me get her a gift or something. Some new draws or something, bro. Sat up there and rubbed her draws all in my face like I'm a punk, or something. Take me to the mall, bro.

LAUGHING SO LOUD AND HARD UNTIL TEARS SPURT OUT OF MY EYES.

"Bro! I'm dead, right now. You killing me with your funnyman act, bro!" BELLY LAUGHING!

"Just take me to the mall, Ace!"

"Man, I ain't taking you to no mall! I ain't thinking about that girl. She is not going to mess with you. She ain't got no brothers. And you can't tell me you didn't enjoy her rubbing her lace underwear in your face, bro.

"I mean, yeah, I liked it. And it wasn't lace; it was silk, bro. But she is still going to kill me or something."

"Bro, come on, man. Stop! What is she gon' do? She ain't no bigger than Janelle Monet, and you running around here scared."

"Man, she crazy. Just take me to the mall. I need to get her a new coat."

"Fool, it's hot outside. And no store in the mall have coats out this time a year. And besides, the mall will be closing in an hour, it will take us an hour alone to get there. The traffic is heavy. It was a huge accident on the way. It's all backed up out there. We can't go to no mall."

"Well, just drop me off at the crib. At least I'll be safe. I gotta out-think her right now. I'm tired anyway. She wore me out. I need to get my mind off of all this. You right, bro. Just take me home. Bidness is picking up, and I can't let her distract me from that. Yeah, take me home, bro. I think I will call it a night."

"Gap, you buggin'. This is me, bro. What's up? You don't bug out like this? What's really going on?"

"What are you talking about, bro? I'm talking about bidness. That's all you know, bro. And you questioning me. You the one that's trippin'."

"Naw. I ain't trippin'. I'm just saying. I thought you might want to hang out tonight, that's all. Our schedule is lean tomorrow. We can take the whole day off."

"That's ok, Ace. Like I told you, I have a headache. Just take me to the crib."

"Whatever, forget you, bro." I mumbled.

It was a surprise to me, and a little hurtful that Gap did not plan a party for me. I tried to act like it didn't bother me. But I was salty. How did I get that wrong? He asked me to take him to Walmart last week, I saw him checking out the party favors. Gap of all people, should have known that my, 'I-don't-care' act, was just that, an act. He knows I be stuntin' when I be acting all hard.

"HOW COULD YOU FORGET MY BIRTHDAY?
HOW COULD YOU!"

"Man Ace, bro. My head is pounding. I feel super sick, bro, like I'mma die. Pull up by Walgreens and get me some Tylenol or Anacin or something."

He popped the top off the bottle and poured four Anacin down his throat without water.

"Bro, hold up." I got out my car again and got him a bottle of water from the trunk. "You ok?" I asked.

85

"Yeah, bro. Just get me home," he said weakly. "Why am I burning up, Ace? What's going on, Ace? My head feels like it's about to explode."

"Don't trip, bro. Just stay calm."

"See, I told you that girl do that Nostradamus, Jedi type stuff. She did something to me, Ace. I know it."

After taking the pills, Gap conked out like a light. He laid his head against the window and didn't say another word. I let him sleep until we pulled up at his house.

"Gap, wake up. You at the cribs, bro. Wake up."

He did not respond.

"Gap, bro? Gap?"

I reached out and shook him. His body felt lifeless.

"Now, I have never seen him sleep this hard before."

"GAP! BROOO!!!"

When he didn't respond, I decided to get out of the car and walk around to the passenger side and wake him that way.

When I made it around to the passenger side of the car, I became increasingly nervous. Gap was still unresponsive to his name or anything that I said to him. His head was still mashed against the window. A thick smudge of Wave Butter where the side of his head was slumping against and sliding down the window was slowly growing and elongating.

"Gap, lean up, bro. Lean up so I can open the door. You hear me? Gap! You at the crib, bro. Wake up, bro."

Gap did not budge. His forehead just hung loosely on the window in the layer of butter and didn't move. I kept thinking, "What is this? This is strange. How did he get this sick so quickly? Maybe that girl did do something to him."

I placed my hand on the door handle and slowly opened the door. Gap's head slumped toward the ground, and his entire body began falling outside the car. I put my knee in the opening so he would not hit the ground.

I did something I don't normally do. I prayed. I'd seen and heard my momma do it enough times. This seemed like one of those 'speak-to-The-Master' moments.

"So, uh, God. What's going on with my guy? Gap, sit up, bro. I can't open the door. You are about to hit the ground. Gap!"

I brushed the falling tears from my eyes with my forearm. I didn't want to deal with the reality of what was happening right in front of me.

"Ok, let me try this again, God. I always thought one of us would get capped in a drive-by or something like that. But this is a good dude. He's getting cut down for nothing. He got a conscience and everything, bro."

Gap was slumping down like a duffle bag, half stuffed with dirty laundry. Gap was dead. I continued pressing my knee against the frame of the car to hold his dead body in place as I opened the door more. He poured out hard like a parachuter whose latch malfunctioned.

"Gap, Gap!" I yelled over and over at the top of my lungs. "No, No, Noooo!" When he didn't answer, I fell to my knees on the ground next to him, still wailing the loss of my friend.

All of the commotion caused Gap's father to exit the house.

I explained that Gap died in my car, and that he thought his girl had Ouija-boarded him and caused him to get deathly ill. Mr. Mensch stared down at his son, slumped over on the ground with a solemn, unyielding look on his face.

"Come on, boy. Let's pick him up and carry him in the house."

While stooping down to lift him, Gap began squirming and coughing faintly.

"Hey, he's moving. He's moving!"

"Ace, help me, bro," Gap whispered feebly. "I'm sick, Ace. What's wrong with me? And, how did I get on the ground? What's going on, Ace?"

Gap tried to lift himself from the ground but couldn't. I can't get up, Ace. I feel weak. I need help. I told you that girl is a witch. She needs her own TV show."

"Yeah, I know, bro. But don't worry, I got you."

"But how did I get out here on the ground, bro? I don't remember getting out of the car, bro."

"Well, he's back," said Mr. Mensch, with a big smile on his face and a sigh of relief. "All that whining. Help the boy up, Ace, so we can get him in the house."

Mr. Mensch and I lifted Gap from the ground, and slowly helped him to the front door and inside the house.

* * * S U R P R I S E * * *

I stopped in my tracks!

"Happy Birthday Ace," was the first thing I saw. It was a cool, handmade banner hanging across the entire wall of the living room. The next thing I saw was a bunch of smiling faces! All my guys and their girls.

Gap and his dad burst into laughter. Gap's girl came and gave him a big kiss and hug!

"Aaaaaah, hahaha! I got you, man! Don't forget, you are also born on April Fool's day, bro! I had to get you!"

All I could do was cover my face in embarrassment and laugh with everyone else. Everybody was in on it; his dad, his girlfriend, my guys. They parked their cars a block away, so I wouldn't catch on!

"Man, Gap, you had me going. Don't EVER do that again! Bro, you had me losing my mind. You had me looking all soft. Got my eyes all sweaty and thangs. Had me out there looking like a chump. You wrong for that."

"Ace, bro, you touched me. You had my back. Y'all, this cat stopped at Walgreens and got me a bottle of Anacin. Y'all should have seen me. I was in there doing some serious Denzel Washington, Academy Award winning performances. I opened the bottle and just started pouring them pills down my throat, no water." Everyone laughed.

"Yeah, y'all should have seen, bro. He poured like half the bottle into his mouth. I thought he was going to OD, or choke to death. I was like, no water... come on bro, ain't nothing that serious. But then this guy just passes out in the car. Let his big greasy, kunk wearing, but no durag having, waveless having, lopsided head, clunked up against my window and greased it all up. Man, I had just got my ride detailed, too!"

Everyone started laughing again.

"I got you bro. You know I ain't going nowhere, no time soon. I saw you that day, peeping me at Walmart. That's why I had to get you, bro. Always trying to outslick somebody. Well, you have just been punked, bro!" Everyone laughed.

NOW, LET'S TURN THIS PARTY UP!

And speaking of party, I got something special for you, Ace. You won't believe it, bro."

BLUFF
ing

SURPRISE!!!

"Nah, nah, nah! This can't be real. You bluffing me. Nah! Bro! You bluffing!"

We walked to the back of the house, and Bluff emerged out of the bedroom and held out both his hands as if to say, "It's me man, in the flesh. Give me a hug."

I looked at Bluff, then Gap, and said, "How, bro? How?"

"Don't worry about how, man. Just know that it is," Bluff said.

The only comeback I had was, "Bro, you tall now! Look at you!"

They busted out laughing.

"So," Bluff said, "Do you plan on having me stand here all night with my arms out, man, acting like you not glad to see your brother, man."

"Bluff... Bro..." I reached out and grabbed him. "My man. Good to see you, bro. So, what's up? It's been like three years. Look at you, bro. You got all tall and thangs. You grew up on ya' boi."

"Maaaan! I'm older than your young butt, anyway. You trippin' Ace."

"Well, I'm out." Gap said. "I'mma let y'all have y'all's family reunion thang. I'mma go join the party again. Get with my girl. Y'all be smooth. Out."

"Out."

"Out."

"Awww man, Bluff, it's good to see you, bro. What have you been up to these past three years, except going to the gym? Maaan, look at you. You on swole and everythang."

92

THE SONG HIS MOTHER SINGS

"Nah, man. I'm chillin'."

"Bet. I know you down there, claiming them streets though."

"Nah, man. That was the plan, but my plans changed. I met a girl. And I think she's the one. The only thing, she is not for the street game, man. I had to make a decision."

"Facts, bro?"

"Yeah, man. I mean, she is THE ONE."

"Well, what's her name."

"Angel, man. Can you believe it? Her name is Angel."

"We always said for us to settle down, God would have to send us an angel."

Laughter fills the hallway where we were standing.

"Yeah Ace, I laid down my playa' card over this one, man. No more double dipping for me. I'm all about my relationship, man. I gave up all this street stuff, man. I went down there and saw a whole new opportunity. I'm in church and everything."

"Whaaat?"

"Bout to be a father and everything, man. And you know I can't be reckless with a lil' shorty, man. It was time for me to do something different."

"You know what, Bluff, I'm proud of you bro, but I thought church boys don't do *that* until they are married? What's up?"

"Thanks, man, and you right. I slipped up, but we got that straight. Now we are waiting until we make everything official."

"That's cool, bro. I feel you – as long as you are serious. You are not bluffing me... are you, bro?"

"Nah, bro. I'm serious as heart surgery. Thanks, man. One thing I have learned is that no one is perfect, and we all can change and make amends for our wrongs. We may not be able to change the past, but we can do what is right as we move forward in life. And that's what I'm doing, man."

"Look at you, Bluff. Sounding all preachery. What, you got one of them backwards collars, bro? You read the bible all day now? What's up?"

Bluff laughs. "Nah man. I'm still me. I'm just growing up. Becoming a man. Sometimes, something will happen in our lives to cause us to shift. For me, it was Angel. She introduced me to Christ. And I have been working on myself ever since. Sometimes, that shift is not so dramatic for some people. Then for others, it's out of this world crazy. But that's what it takes for them to step into their greatness. But either way, when that time comes, they know it."

"Hmmm. That's interesting, bro. You sound like my mom. She is always preaching about how great I am supposed to be, but I don't have a clue what it is. I wonder when mine will come. I need to do something different, bro. I'm serious."

"Ok, ok. What about your girl? Let's start with THAT! Are you still with your girl?"

I look at him sideways. "Bro, who is you talkin' bout?"

"Stop playing, man. You know the one I'm talking about, the one with all the brothers. She used to have you in check! What was her name, Sheila?"

"Shaquita, bro. And no, bro. I ain't thinking about that girl. And she didn't have me in check, bro. I checked her!"

"Whatever man," Bluff said, laughing and shaking his head.

"And ain't nobody scared of her brothers, bro. I'll knock them fools out!"

"Ok. You da' man."

"But nah, bro. I ain't thinking about no girls right now. Shaquita is cool. I told her to finish school and make something of her life. You know she is a junior in college, bro."

"Man, I don't know how you do it. You always did pull them cougars, man."

"Yeah, bro. I'm a cougar magnet or something."

We laugh again.

"But I ain't thinking about them cougars either, bro. I'm building my business."

"I feel you, man. But anyway, we gotta do something before I pull out."

"Ok, cool, cool, cool. How long are you staying in town, bro?"

"Just two weeks, man. I gotta get back to my life, man. I think I am going to pop the question when I get back. I'm telling you, man. She is the one!"

"I feel you, bro. And you make sure you be there for your lil' shorty. You already know my situation, how my mom did me."

"Man! Don't tell me you are still on that? I thought we cleared that up years ago. Wow! You need to let that go. You can't keep blaming your mother for your father not being in your life. Look, a real man will handle his own business. He will make a way to be in his child's life, regardless of what the mother says or does. He is the father and has rights. The law is on his side when it comes to that. You need to stop pinning that on your mom, man."

"Whatever, bro. My mom be buggin'."

"Listen, man. Who knows? The time may come when you may actually meet your father, and you might end up realizing that your mom did you a favor, man. Your mom has done nothing but pour love down on you ever since I have known you, man. So, just based on that alone, I say whatever she has or has not done concerning your dad, is all love, man. You gotta give her that, man."

"Come on bro... when you say you leaving?..."

"Oh, it's like that. huh?"

We start sparring right there in the hallway, like we used to do back in the day.

"Ah haaa! You taller now, but I still got them hands, bro." I weaved and bobbed, and did my slick footwork and left ole Bluff wondering what angle I was coming at him from. I started mimicking the cowardly lion from *The Wiz*. "Put 'em up, put 'em up. I'll fight you with one paw tied behind my back. I'll fight you standing on one foot. I'll fight you with my eyes closed. Oooh, pull an ax on me, ay. Well, put 'em up, put 'em up..."

We laughed and laughed.

"Man, we have a lot of catching up to do," Bluff said.

"Yeah bro, it's been three years. How's your mom doing?"

"She's doing good, man. She's in church, too. She's off that stuff and everything, man. We are making it work. She can't wait to be a grandma, man!"

"That's what's up, bro. I'm really happy for you, Bluff."

"Yeah man, but I need you to do me a favor."

"Anything, bro. I got you. Just let me know, and it's done."

Bluff started laughing.

"What are you laughing for, bro? What's funny, bro?"

"Nah, it's nothing, man. You just gon' trip out when I tell you my favor."

I start laughing even before he tells me. "Just spit it bro. What's up?" I said with a large radiator grin splashed all over my face.

"Man, Ace. I need you to take me to the spot, man. I want to go stand around and listen to the guys tell their wild stories, man."

"You crazy, bro. I still go down there a couple times a week myself, bro, and I don't even know why. I don't believe nothing they be saying. They know they be some lying fools!"

"Yup. Maybe so, Ace... but I know you've heard the saying that the truth is stranger than fiction. Well... there you go!"

"Bro, if those stories are true, those old cats need to be thrown under the jail or in the loony bin."

We start laughing again.

"Ace, you funny, man. A lot of them have been to jail and have already paid for their crimes. So, some of what they say is real."

"Listen to you, Bluff. You really believe this stuff. Well, I'm tired, bro. Let me go out here and say good night to all my friends. But this really has been the best celebration ever, bro. Let me take care of my thank-yous and good-nights. I have some business I have to square away tomorrow and the day after. But after that, I will be free. It will be nice to hang out at the spot, bro. That's where it all began. But anyway, don't go soft on me. Don't go down memory lane, bringing up the good ole days. Wow! Where has the time gone? But like I said, give me a day or so, and I'll be back."

"Cool, cool, cool. Plus, my pops has a new girl he wants me to meet."

I start laughing. "Yeah, I know. Gap said she looks like a shark, bro!"

"Yeah, that's Gap for you. He knows how to talk about my father's women. But hey, pops is going to do pops.

"I already know. But hey, bro, I really am glad to see you, Bluff.

"Me too, Ace. I'm glad to see you too."

"Cool, let me handle this, and I will see you in a day or so. I'll call you if the plans change."

Swept
AWAY

"MOMMA!" I yelled out over and over. "AVIA! Where are you? I know you hear me calling you," I said as I made my way to the back porch.

"Didn't you hear me calling you, lil girl? I'm hungry. Go fix me some pancakes and bacon! And why are you back here sweeping this porch? We don't even use this porch! I have things to do, and you are wasting time, making me late for my appointments. I need you to iron my shirt. Let's go. MOVE IT. I have places to go and people to do. Move it! Move it! Let's go!"

Momma continued sweeping. "Are you going to school today, Aaron? It's already 10 A.M."

"Stop asking dumb questions, stupid. You do that on purpose, trying to make me mad! Well, it's not going to work. I am not going to get swept away in your mess today. GO FIX MY FOOD!!! And get my clothes ready. I told you yesterday, right before I walked out the door, that I would be back at 10 A.M., this morning. I told you to have breakfast and my clothes ready. What's the point of being my mother if you can't get simple instructions right, Avia? And what are you sweeping so hard for? You are asking for these hands..."

I poked her on the side of her head, next to her temple. "Think, Avia! Stop standing there staring at me. STOP SWEEPING! GO FIX MY FOOD! IRON MY SHIRT! It's simple mathematics. 1.2.3."

She shuffled away as quickly as she could and didn't say a word. She went into the kitchen to start preparing my pancakes.

I gave her a swift kick to her scrawny behind then stormed behind her angrily barking out orders. "Get the bacon out of the freezer. EVERYBODY KNOWS you have to cook the meat first, Avia! I muffed her in the face. Bacon takes longer than pancakes. How dumb are you?"

I snatched the bacon out of the freezer, then threw the frozen pack of bacon on the stove and turned the fire up to high. I grabbed the back of her head and neck and forced it down toward the pan.

"You see, lil' girl! I can light up your whole raggedy face right now!"

She tried to wiggle away but I gripped her neck tighter. "Where you going, lil girl? Huh? You can't get away from me. What you gon' do?"

She squealed.

"That's right, squeal like a little piglet. I can light up your world. But it won't make no difference. You can't get any uglier!" I let her go. "Now get to cooking!"

She grabbed her black cast iron skillet from the dish rack and placed it on the stove. I threw the frozen slab into that skillet when she removed the smaller one from the fire. It was thawing in the plastic packaging and dripping, but I didn't care. Liquid bacon fat flung everywhere when I tossed the cooking plastic into the skillet. I left the fire on high. "And you better not burn it. And why are you trying to fry bacon while it is frozen and still in the plastic, stupid?"

"Aaron, baby, why are you coming in here with this foolishness this morning? Go on upstairs so I can fix your food, baby. It won't take but a minute."

"Don't 'son' and 'baby' me! You slipping, Avia. You slipping bad." I pointed my fingers like a pistol and thrusted the side of her temple again. "It's time for me to take out the trash and put you in the old folk's home. That's why I'm coming in here with this foolishness! You are old, lil' girl, and you always lying. Even a bunch of drunks standing on the corner next to a liquor store got more truth in 'em than you. At least I can believe them. But I can't believe nothing that comes out of your mouth. And this is how I know when you are lying, Avia... your mouth moves. That's how I know. Every time you open your mouth, a lie rockets out of it."

Momma ignored me. She took the bacon off the fire and put it back in the freezer and got the open pack of bacon from the meat tray of the refrigerator and put six slices in the cast iron skillet and turned the heat down to medium, then began singing her song... "Lord Don't Move My Mountain..."

"And stop singing that blasted song. I've been hearing it all my life. It's a ridiculous song and makes no sense at all. I'm going upstairs. When I get back, you better have my food ready."

I stormed upstairs and took a shower. When I came back down the stairs, Momma had everything laid out as if I hadn't muttered one contentious word or hand to her.

My food was garnished on my special china, accompanied by my special silverware. She had two sets of clothes for me to choose from, pressed and creased, laid out on the sofa, waiting for me slip into one or the other.

But Momma was nowhere around.

I could hear her on the back porch. She was singing her song while she swept away the remaining leaves.

"STOP SINGING THAT SONG!" I yelled! "Wasting time back there on that porch. You need to be out there on the corner with all those other drunk fools. Maybe you will get swept away with all the curbside trash. You will be lying in your grave. And that can't come quick enough for me."

AAAAAVIA!

"I know you hear me calling you! Come here, old lady! AVIA!... Man, forget you, fool! I ought to come back there and kill you. Snuff you out like you snuffed my dad out of my life! Just die already, old lady. Just die!"

DOOR SLAMS!

After the door slams, she makes her way back to the front of the house and cleans up the dishes and puts away the untouched breakfast she prepared with love.

Tired and overcome with grief, her battered body is further plagued with the pitiless pangs of my contentious words. Relinquishing to the heavy weight of defeat, slowly, she shuffles to the living room and takes needed rest in the gloved comfort of her merciful Lazy Boy.

With defeated and exhaustive tears lamenting perilously down her anguishing face, lugubriously she reflects over her broken life and prays magnificently...

Father, in The Name of Jesus...

(Weeping sorely...)

HE IS MY SON.

HE IS MY SON.

He's all I got in this world.

He's all I have.

I don't have anything else.

Lord, he's my darling.

My son.

My only child.

He's the joy of my life;

The brightest sunshine in my day.

My very reason for inhaling.

I can't exhale without him.

I can't breathe.

You loaned him to me,

This, my bundle of joy,

And placed his heart in my heart.

His soul in my soul,

In my guardianship,
And in my care.
He's clovered in my love.
Wreathed and wrapped and woven in incessant
motherly worry from
Wake to wait.
18 years unconditionally.
I am his,
And he is mine,
And I am ever so fond of him,
His eyes,
His smile,
His sense of humor,
His laughter,
His independence,
His drive...
BUT LORD, HE MAKES ME CRY!
He yells,
And curses.
I've tried my best to do right by him,
But he has been more than I allow.
He is a lot, Lord. He is too much.
He's oppositional.
And mean.
If I have faltered in the slightest of ways,
Or have been destitute in this honorable duty in
the smallest degree,
Wash me.
Where I am partaker in his waywardness in
anywise, Dear Lord,
Lay it not to his charge.

Cleanse me.
Cleanse my heart.
I am his mother,
And sole guardian.
And I have thought myself accursed at times.
Forgive me,
For I am broken.
I am a broken woman.
Make me whole.
Any weakness, which causeth him to be
miscreant,
Lay it upon me.
Allow his misconduct to be mine to bear.
There is deficiency within him,
Because deficiency has grown within me, within
my reigns.
Be Thou Merciful,
Thou Merciful God.
Hold not this fracture to his charge.
HE IS MY SON.
How shall I ever rest,
Or shall I ever have peace,
When he is tormented?
Even as The Prophet Jeremiah wails aloud, so
does my soul wail for my only begotten.
The love of my youth.
The love of my loins.
OHH, OHH, OH, OH.
HE IS MY SON!
HE IS MY SON!
I am maddened by reason of grief.

Sanity forsakes me.
Lucidity eludes me.
Words leave me.
Ugggggggggg.
Yellow bitterness usurps my words.
I gurgle in silence alone.
Hearken unto the language of the grieved.
Gurgle.
Cough.
Grieve.
Exiled. Muted. Paused. Speechless.
Ugggggggggg.
Strong, pungent heaving.
Vomit in silence, alone.
Sick in the stomach.
Quiet madness.
Coughing.
Choking.
Pain.
Delirious pain.
Heave.
Grieve.
Throw up.
Lean forward,
Head toward the floor.
Floor splattered in chuck.
My tongue cleaveth to the roof of my mouth.
Ohhhhhhhh.
SPEAK LORD...
　　　　Speak to your storm, child.
A faint whisper in the belly of my soul declares...

HE IS MY SON.
PUKE...
And I love him.
PUKE...
LORD...
HE IS MY SON.
I love him.
PUKE...
An hour passes
Then two
Then three.
This poor woman cried...
PUKE...
PUKE...
PUKE...
HE IS MY SON.
Over and Over.
Again, and Again.
Without Fail.
HE IS MY SON.
PUKE...
He is willful,
And wouldest not hear.
He won't listen,
But I love him, Lord.
I love him, hard as cement.
As an unsolved mystery.
I love him like nothing.
And I pray You do too.
Love him, Lord.
Love my son.

Love him to wholeness.
This is his mother's plea,
Even my very last will and testament.
To You, I Owe All.
All I have is my son.
Take Him as Your own.
He is Yours.
You said so.
You declared so.
I can do nothing more than cry for him.
PUKE
CHUCK
OOOOH OOOOOH
I weep.
I mourn.
I sob sorely.
I make a river to wear grooves in my face.
I squint my eyes tightly,
And rub them with the balls of my hands.
My eyes are red.
Stinging.
Restless.
Broken sore.
They are ridden with worry.
The rain burrows a hole deep within my soul.
I wail and drool and quiver and ache and gush
water from my eyes.
Sound words leave my mind.
Mmmmmm.
Let these, his mother's tears,
Reach Your Merciful Throne,

And pity, I pray they obtain.
Lord, he's my child.
My nestling.
My baby.
He is my fry, my tike, my boy.
My fetus, yes.
My little one, also yes.
No one nowhere pities him.
My eyes are his only pity.
My tears are unwed, solitaire, unattached.
If mine eyes weep not for him,
None eye will...
Mine eyes are built for weeping.
They are built to wail,
To howl.
To lament.
Whimper.
Caterwaul.
Squawk.
CRY.
My water flows.
My river runs.
My sea floods.
The gates of my center have washed ashore.
Forgive him, Lord.
HE IS MY SON.
He is an ornery child.
Sandbagged ever before he was
Born dastardly,
But God, O Merciful King,
I wail at your feet.

I lay at Your Passageway
That You mayest see me wail
When You pass by.
The old hymnal from my childhood rose within
me to comfort my pain.
Pass me not, O gentle Savior
This sublime request was the only sentiment.
All my emotions aligned themselves accordingly.
Hear my humble cry,
While on others Thou art calling,
Do not pass me by.
HE IS MY SON.
Savior, Savior,
Hear my humble cry,
While on others Thou art calling,
Do not pass me by.
Save him, God.
There is much words cannot convey.
For my overflowing oculi are
cruelly connected to
Yosemite
Niagara
Skogafoss
Angel
Iguazu
HE SCARES ME.
His hands are become a slap in my face.
He brushes against me roughly with his shoulder.
Sticks his foot out as I pass by;
Laughs when I fall.
He uses his tongue as a dagger.

Dirty Bastard.

Nasty Slut.

Ugly Whore.

Liar.

She-devil.

Stripper.

Skank.

Avia.

But it hurts most of all when he calls me little girl.

Obviously, he hates me.

HELP ME LOVE HIM.

He says he will be glad when I'm gone for good.

He's going to kill me, God.

WHY...

WHY DOES HE HATE ME?

And I love him, still?

Oh God...

If I could steal away with him just once.

I'd tell him all my heart.

Let him hear my love.

I live only to love him.

Hurt so he may heal.

Deny my value,

That he may discover his worth.

He is my son.

Fix his heart, God.

Heal his pain.

That he may find his place in this world.

He's reckless, Lord.

He sells drugs.

Hurts women.

Hurts men.
Hurts children.
His voice travels down the stairs,
Straight into my heart like a kukri blade.
I bleed.
He lies.
I'm chained.
He's charming.
I'm silenced.
He's seductive.
He dials their numbers and deceives them all.
But I know him.
He knows I know him.
My days are numbered with him.
He's a most formidable child.
Unrepentant.
But don't destroy him, Lord.
Please untether him from inherent sin,
For he is a sinner inherently.
It is not his fault.
Wash him down to his thoughts.
I never thought it would be like this.
His thoughts are not my thoughts.
His thoughts are unwashed.
Unswept. Ungarnished. Unhinged. Unusual.
Untimely. Unmourned. Understood.
But I need some understanding.
I pray for his soul without ceasing.
Yet, he is maculate.
And I'm tired.
I am infirmed.

Purge him from the feral man.
Protect him.
Heal his mind.
Heal his spirit.
And for everything he has ever done,
I FORGIVE HIM, because,
HE IS MY SON.

6+2x4-3

IT'S
WHO

I
AM

Bluff and I are fired up and excited about our drive to Bello Heights. We talked trash and real-talk all the way there. Well, I talked most of the trash, and Bluff, well, he kept it 100.

I was glad to have Bluff home, even if it was just for a couple of weeks. He was different, but not really. He had given up the street life, but somehow, I still knew that I could count on him.

I was fascinated by his change. He and I had made so many plans back in the day about being in business together and building an empire, but that seems like a lifetime ago. We are now a world apart. Bluff is doing his own thing. He is in church now. He has found The Lord. Good for him. He is about to be a father, get married to an angel, and who knows, he may even become a big-time preacher one day. I can't be mad at him for that. This dream was never his. It was always mine. He's found what he was looking for, something that I have wished for all my life:

PEACE.

I ain't got that.

I wish I did.

But I don't.

Besides, I don't need it.

I got what I need:

Guns.

Bodies.

Clout.

A reputation in these streets.

Connections.

Power.

Authority.

Respect.

Yeah.

I got respect.

I don't know how he laid this life down. It's all we talked about. But aaee, to each his own.

I looked over at him, and he was just laughing, grinning and ranting on and on about how he couldn't wait to get out there and just chill with those old cats. He was really into it.

I smiled, then lifted up my armrest and laid a yellow envelope on the seat.

He looked at me, and I gave him the nod. He picked it up and opened it.

It was 50 bands.

"$50,000, Ace? Are you serious? I can't take this money, man."

"Why not?"

"It's 50Gs, that's why not. How will I get the cash to pay this back? I don't hustle anymore, Ace."

"Come on, bro. Don't insult me. Who said anything about paying me back? You didn't ask for this, JUST LIKE YOU DIDN'T ASK ME TO BE YO' LIL' SHORTY'S GUARDIAN-DADDY WHEN HE GET HERE, BRO. WHAT'S UP WITH THAT?"

"Man, that goes without saying. You already know. Our plans have not changed. We said we would look out for each other and our kids! That's what it is. That will never change. And when you decide to settle down and stop dogging all these girls and go get your

'Angel,' I got you too, man. But what about this cash? I ain't got no money!"

"It's a gift, bro. I got you. I will always have you. You are family to me. And to be honest with you bro, I'm glad you are not out here. This life was never for you, bro. You were always better than this. It's like you are the good part of me that I always wanted to find, but it's just not in me."

"Nah man, you are better than this."

"Not me, bro. I was born here."

"Man, what are you talking about? You were born in Chainey Hospital, on the Northside."

"Bro! You not listening. Stop playing and listen to me. I'm being 100 right now, bro. Up North, Down South, Out West, Eastside. Don't none of that matter, bro!"

"Ok man. I feel you. I'm all ears."

"Good fool, because I'm talking about the gutter, bro. These streets. I'm a child of the streets, a man of the wild. I'm a lowlife thug. It's who I am. Just like my pops, bro. How do you bring a child into this world and just leave him out here in these streets to get pissed on, bro? What kind of lowdown do you have to be to do some messed up stuff like that? Forget that sucka, bro. And that's why I rain down on all these fools. LOVE NONE, BRO."

"I feel you, man. I feel you."

"This, out here, has been my home, bro. You feel me? These streets is my castle. This is where I'm from. I don't know nothing else, bro. I ain't nothing at the crib, but I'm the king out here, bro. I'm KING. So, I choose this. I choose this bull crap, man. I can do this crap with my

eyes closed. 2:03 A.M. on the dot. I can do it with one
hand tied behind my back. Put 'em up..."

"Aaaah, you funny, man."

"But seriously, bro, 50 bands ain't nothing to me.
I'll make that back before we eat lunch today. My soldiers
are posted up even as we speak. I ain't doing nothing but
getting paid."

"Ooooh, you got it like DAT?"

"That's right, bro. I got it like DAT! WE got it like
dat!" We both laughed.

"Well, I feel you, Ace. I am proud of you man. I'm
proud that you have proven to yourself that you can do
whatever you set your mind to do. I'm just hoping you will
one day make your mind up to leave all this alone. The
system is so crooked, I won't even begin to talk about not
using dirty money. You can make money and be safe all at
the same time, man. Why? Cuz we brothers. That's why."

I smiled and sighed. "Yeaaah, we started this
empire together, bro. We are not just out there on the
streets like we envisioned initially. You know I'm gifted
with those computers, bro. I use technology to move our
products, bro. That app we were working on is in full play,
bro. It's a seamless transition. And nobody is out there
getting their hands dirty. Well, we still have soldiers out
there on the street, you know. Any money is plenty
money. It's just my way of giving back. So, those 50 bands
is the least I can do. Think of it as an early wedding
present."

"Well, we did say we were going to do it. And look
at you – you did it, man. Just remember Ace, man, I'm
here for you too. And don't forget what else we said."

THE SONG HIS MOTHER SINGS

"And what's that, bro?"

"You know, Ace. We always said that we would not stay in this life forever. We were just trying to build a better life for ourselves, beat the system and rain down on *it* for a change."

"Yeah, that's true, bro. You know the game, Bluff. Once you taste this money, bro, it sucks you in like a vacuum. I can't get out, bro. If I get out, what else do I have? I ain't got nothing else. This is who I am. I'm glad you got out though. I will always have your back, Bluff, and my lil' nephew when he gets here, bro."

"That's love, man. Thanks Ace. But please know this, it's not too late for you either. You can still get out too. It's not too late."

"Bluff, bro. It's too late for me. I'm hooked. I'm a junkie to this life. I'm a slave to it. When I die, I'mma die right here in my castle, bro. You know what they say, 'there's no place like home!'"

Then there was a long silence between us filled with nothing but awkwardness.

"Look man," Bluff finally said. He was pointing across the street at the drunks. "Man, we in here reminiscing and thinking so hard, we passed up the spot. Let me turn around so I can park on the same side of the street."

We didn't park directly on the corner. We generally saved the first two or three parks for cats that would generally grab and go. We parked a few more spaces down the street, close enough to be in eyeshot but far enough away where the drunks and winos wouldn't know to ask for a ride.

121

Bluff was rubbing his hands and smiling as we got closer to the dreams-deferred corner.

"Bluff, you acting like we're about to go meet some fine women or something." I started laughing, then reached for my brush and hit my waves a few times. "You are a little too geeked up for me, bro. Turn that down, bro. You making me nervous." Bluff started laughing.

"Nah, Ace. You geeked up too. Don't think I don't know that you still come down here and chill with these old dudes. Like I said, the stories are entertaining, but they are deep also. Being around these cats is like being in live theater. You know this is what's up, man."

"Whatever, bro. You trippin'."

Anything goes in Bello Heights
Bello Heights is where local scum bags swarm in droves.
It's where human swine prey,
And preachers never pray.
It's a place where charlatans creep in the crouching position capturing conscienceless connivers off guard in their carnal conjugal cycle of uncompromising charm.
It's a place where carnivores devour unhatched eggs,
Embryos never mature,
No matter how young or old.
Dreams die there.
Visions go blind.
It's a place where good girls aren't for long;
They have sex with many men but have never made love to any man.
Bello Heights isn't a place for making love.
It makes no sense.
It makes addicts.
It's a place for cokeheads,
Meth heads,
Crackheads.
But not level heads.
It's a place for riffraff and goodfellas.
Hypes and hypocrites.
It's a place for reprobates,
Not rebates,
You put your whole soul in
And never holdback.

But they always holdout.
You are the one on a payment plan
It's a place where backsliders slide.
Junkies never get clean.
The high are always low.
It's a place where psychics suffer from psychosis,
Doctors are hypochondriacs who medicate their
ills with placebos.
Everyone medicates in Bello Heights,
And everyone has a place to lay their head:
A sidewalk,
Slumped over on a dumpster,
Molded seats of an abandoned car,
A wet street curb,
The street itself,
A pothole becomes your pillow,
A cardboard box,
A vacant building,
An alley,
Old tarps found drifting in the wind,
The viaduct under the train tracks,
Yes, Bello Heights is a real motel.
It's a family of decadent discards, dope fiends,
drunks and demimondes.
It's a place where whores are ladies,
Of the night, of course.
It's a place where men and little boys are
also ladies of the night.
A place where little girls are trained to be Cougars
that hunt grown men as easily as finding eggs in
the backyard on Easter Sunday.

The girls are young in Bello Heights.
Some are older,
By the time they are 14, 15, they are grown
anyway, and know all the tricks.
The men are mid-50s to 80s.
But no matter their age,
all of them like the young girls most of all.
Even the young men like the girls.
But many of the young men choose the Cougars
because it's more money in it for them.
And it's even more money when they choose
the men.
The mothers of Bello Heights train the young
girls well.
"Rule number one and number two," she says.
"Get the money and don't get killed."
Many of the girls fail at both.
That's just the thing in Bello Heights.
You see a girl today, she goes into an alley, or
hops into a car...
She failed at both rule number one and rule
number two.
But there's always another little girl or little boy
to fail at rule number one and rule number two.
You could always tell by the clickety-clackety
beat on the pavement,
or the partially surviving sidewalk,
that a new girl was arriving in Bello Heights.
But it wasn't long before her clickety-clack was
silent as all the other worn gym shoes and bare

feet in Bello Heights.
She learned quickly, to move in silence.
Only when working at the edge of Bello Heights
did her feet clickety-clack.
All the stores had long stopped being stores. They
were storefronts for other businesses,
you know, red light, green light,
only there were no green lights in this district.
Men did business with women, girls and boys, as
long as his skin was soft and supple like biscuit
dough.
Sometimes it was rough and hairy.
They pay good money for rough and hairy.
In Bello Heights, psychopaths, sociopaths,
schizophrenics, your bipolars, the ungovernables,
the deranged, the scum of the earth, are
welcome...
It's home for good or they can take permanent
part-time residence in the guest quarters,
depending upon their agenda.
But eventually, every local unsavory finds their
way to Bello Heights,
one way or the other.
And everyone is safe,
if they keep their ear to the ground and sleep
with one eye open.

There are lots of stores in Bello Heights.
Bello Heights is really just one long strip of
starving businesses and starving rejects with a
short bend at both ends,

also flooded with starving rejects and starving
businesses.
Most of the businesses are out of business,
but lots of cash is still made, taken, stolen and
invested in Bello Heights.
Dirty rejects spend money, and dirty rejects make
money.
The unusual smell in Bello Heights is usually
familiar to newcomers.
Just inhale in any public bathroom.
That's the essence of Bello Heights.
The aromatic flower,
The delicate driftings,
The fragrance that wafts.
 It's the air we breathe in Bello Heights.
But you get used to it, ignore it, or if you are a
true decadent, you crave it.
Your body quakes for it.
The stench comes in many varieties:
You have your browns, your pale yellows, your
reds, and your pale, grayish-whites,
And there's worse crap than that.
Bello Heights is a crap gold mine.
You have the crap that men tell women and
women tell men in Bello Heights.
You have the crap the police do in Bello Heights.
The decadents and batches of deplorables inhale
deeply the twang of ill repute, lawfulness,
lawlessness, and a number two...
It all smells the same in Bello Heights.
Recidivism stinks in Bello Heights.

Relapsers and repeat offenders
stink in Bello Heights.
Little girls in high heels and stockings stink.
Men that look at them with lust in their eyes
stink.
Squalor stinks.

> "Momma, what is squalor?"
> "I don't know what squalor is, child. I
> think it's something you can get paid for."
> "But does it stink?"
> "I think so, but I'm not sure. You gotta do
> what you gotta do..."

Hot ghetto mess stinks,
But so does white supremacy.
That has a real stench,
Like a white toilet seat,
Or a white lie.
White lies really stink.
Bulimia stinks.
Hunger stinks everywhere.
White coats stink.
Psychobabble reeks.
Sex trafficking stinks,
But a lot of rich people like how it smells.
The Link card stinks,
And most of us know why.
This is America! That's Why!
IGNORANCE STINKS!
I wish it didn't stink so much.
Some people are born smelling like that.

You just gotta pray for them, and get them
cleaned up.
Cause if not, they will stink worse and worse.
Dual diagnosis stink.
Black Male is a dual diagnosis.
That makes me sad, because it really doesn't
stink. They just say it stinks.
Politics, Government, and State Laws
all stink.
Jail stinks because of crooked judges,
Judges stink because of payoffs and white males
that blackmail.
Black males stink mostly because of white males
controlling the citadel.
But they say business is good.
Rape stinks.
Statutory rape stinks the same.
Consensual sex with a minor?
How is that consensual?
Widespread stinks.
"Momma, why are you crying?"
"Because I'm happy."
"Why are you happy, Momma?"
"Your daddy died."
Deadbeats have a life of their own,
But now, he shares it with you.
Two are better than one.
Momma stinks all by herself.
Insurrection stinks.
Madmen in power stink.

And one madman alone can stink up a whole
house, but it may take 4 years
The reds have the blues.
The blues are ready to slay.
But the blacks are told to stop crying and
Wipe the tear gas from their eyes.
How sinister.
The wages of sinister is death.
Nothing's more sinister than sin.
Death is better than life,
If it's not number 2.
Urban stinks.
Recurring incidents have a malodor.
Foul play stinks.
R Kelly stinks.
Harvey Weinstein smells like crap.
Bill Cosby was funny as crap.
All Lives Matters is a dirty trick,
and a whole bunch of crap against Black Lives that
really do matter.
George Floyd's life did matter!
Say his name!
Emmet Till! Sandra Bland! Say their names!
Joe Biden and Kamala Harris matter.
Barack and Michelle Obama matter.
They don't stink.
Black Wall Street and what happened to it,
matters a lot.
Say the names of the bloody backs and broken
spirits that built America.
SAY ALL THEIR NAMES

La Amistad, Duc du Maine, Isabella, and Joaquina
carried their names thousands of miles from the
free shores of Africa to bondage and servitude of
the land of the "free" and the home of the brave
in America.
But their names are written in blood and
permanently soaked in the wood grain of ships
and minds of the guilty.
AFRICA LIVES!
She lives in America.
Discovered America,
And built America.
Just admit it.
The Truth will set you free.
Break from your chains of denial,
Chains that you wear since The Nile.
Most predators deny any wrongdoings.
That's because they are full of crap.
Liars don't admit they stink;
They just keep craping.
MeToo, I agree that liars stink.
They stink up the place
Like many other men of position.
They deny all accusations, then, in coward's
fashion, resign.
That really stinks.
They should be in jail,
But instead, they are in Bello Heights.
WELCOME TO BELLO HEIGHTS...

Something
NEW
on memory lane

We passed up several drunks as we walked down the block. None of them looked familiar to Bluff.

"Man, Ace. I don't know half these dudes anymore."

"Yeah Bluff, a lot of them are new, but you still know quite a few. Look over there. You know all of those cats. And look at him, right there, bro. I know you remember him. What's his name?"

"Who? The old cat right there? Man, I don't know that old dude."

"Yes, you do, bro. Look again."

"Wait, I think you're right. I know him, Ace. You're right, man. He does look familiar. Let me think. What is his name? Nah, man, that can't be who I think it is. Is that Candyman?"

"Yup!"

Proud of his memory moment, Bluff had a big old first-grade smile on his face.

"See, bro, your memory is still straight. Talking like you have Alzheimer or dementia or something. You know these cats."

"Yeah, I guess I do."

"Candyman is right here every time I come. Bro, I think he lives down here. And he still asks about you, too. He may not recognize you though, since you got your height and your beard and thangs, and that big jug head up there wobbling on your neck!"

"Wow! You got jokes! But look at him, man. Candyman has aged. I really did not recognize him. Is he sick or something? He doesn't look like himself."

"Stomach cancer, bro."

"Wow. And he still comes down here every day and drinks."

"Ay, you know these old cats. Candyman is as wild as they come. He said he can't beat cancer, so if he can't go down fighting, he may as well go down drunk as a skunk! I told you, the old man is crazy. But I feel him, though."

"Man, I feel you. I just hate to hear that, man."

"Ay, you know how these cats are. They are out here every day, going down memory lane, feeling like they have nothing to live for and nothing to die for. It is what it is, bro. You already know. Well anyway, let me holla at him. What's up, Candyman? What's up, mane?"

"Aaay, Ace!" Candyman responds, "What's up, youngsta?"

"Nothing to it, mane. Still out here puttin' in work. You know me."

"Alright then, youngsta. That's what I like to hear."

"But hey, Candyman, I got someone I want you to see. Look who's here, mane!" I step to the side, and Bluff takes a few steps forward.

Candyman's eyes light up! "Aaaay everybody, look who's here!" Everyone's eyes follow the excitement in Candyman's voice. "It's Bluff! Y'all remember lil' shorty. If my memory serves me correctly, he used to catch the bus down here every day and just hang out with us. He didn't have much to say, until one day he unloaded on us like he had just dodged a good behind beatin' from his

momma! The boy wouldn't stop talking after that!"
Everyone started laughing!

A couple of the other cats remember him as well.
They greeted him with warm smiles, accelerated laughter,
pats on the back and handshakes. Bluff was feeling like a
true celebrity.

"Look at you, bro," I said to Bluff, "Back on the
scene and blowing up already! You are a star, Bluff. A star
out here on the corner!"

"Ace, you are crazy! Just shut up, man."

As usual, we start laughing.

"Where have you been, mane?" Candyman asked.
"It's been a while since you stopped through to see us,
mane. You been locked up? We try to tell you young cats
about that fast life. But see son, that's your problem. You
don't listen."

Bluff and I looked at one another and started
laughing because we knew it was about to be on.

"Ace, I thought you said he wouldn't recognize
me."

"Ay bro, maybe you are right. Maybe these cats
are sharper than I thought. But I don't know, he's asking
about jail. I told him you and your mom moved out of
town. Then he said you used to catch the bus, but you had
your own ride. So, maybe it's a 50/50 shot. Sometimes
their brains kick in, sometimes they don't!" We started
laughing and were already having a great time.

There were several new faces in the crowd. One
in particular stood out. Bluff and I noticed him when he
was walking down the street in our direction. He was

clean, dressed to a tee, like he was a playa' or something. His presence commanded attention.

All eyes were on him, including mine.

He looked like he knew something the rest of the world didn't know... like he was on a mission, and I was curious to find out what it was. His swag was mysterious and had me guessing what was up.

I wondered what his intentions were. *What's up, old man? I see you. What are you on? A smooth old cat like you... you ain't no regular drunk. What do you want? Old cats like you are always on something. I know you are not out here on this corner just to chew the fat. So, what's the skinny, old man?*

Although he was an old dude, he looked younger than the other winos, which were all in their late 60s and 70s and beyond. This dude was barely hitting 50 or 55. He was too clean to be an ordinary run-of-the-mill kind of drunk. That's what caught my attention.

Look like these old cats' antennas would have gone up just like mine, but everyone else in the crowd just seemed enamored by his curbside appeal. They were sitting around blowing him up, whispering under their breath about how clean he was.

I mean, sure, his presence would attract some attention. But not like that. All of a sudden, these drunk fools act like they are sober now just because of this guy. I mean, really?

I was just as clean as he was, and I was better looking. But no one made that big a deal over me when I first stepped up to the corner.

He was stepping into the light and taking all my shine. It made me wonder what he had that I didn't have. But I guess I couldn't lie to myself... all that attention they poured on him made me a little salty. All he did was walk up on the scene. There have been several times where I shared love with the entire corner and purchased drinks for everyone. But now, they are out here drooling over this cat.

I whispered to Bluff, "Who is this old cat, man? Coming out here taking all the light. I don't like him, bro."

Bluff nodded.

There was something about him. It was too early for me to put my finger on the exact issue, but I was definitely curious to find out what he was about. *Walking up on my corner with that smug look on your face. I ought to come over there and slap it off. See how you like that, chump.*

"Yeah, I don't like this guy, Bluff. Did you see how he walked up here on us like he owns this corner? Coming through here like he's Humphrey Bogart or something and just gon' bogart his way to a seat at the table. What? Does he plan on evicting us and becoming the King over the corner? So what, is he the 'Corner King' now?"

Bluff listened to what I had to say and smiled as he tried to process it. I turned back to the new guy.

"We started all this, Bluff. We are the kings out here on this corner, bro."

Bluff continued listening to me rant about the new guy.

"I will find out, Bluff. You watch, bro. I'mma find out what he's up to."

Bluff turned to me and said, "Hmmm," with a slight smile on his face.

"I see you smiling, bro, but I am serious. This dude is on something, Bluff."

Again, I had to admit to myself that I was feeling a little jealous. Not even Bluff was taking me seriously. There was something admirable about that old cat. Maybe that is why even Bluff wasn't saying anything. I could even feel myself about to be sucked into his funnel of worship. But I wasn't having it. Bluff and the rest of these fools could be all Marshall Applewhitishly if they want, but I wasn't about to jump on that wagon.

I see you, old man. I don't know you, but I got to give it to you. Coming through here all brand-new looking, dazzling all these fools. You smooth. I'll give you that, and I know you gave up a good penny for those Cesare Paciotti knockoffs. How do I know that they knockoffs? CAUSE I HAVE THAT SAME PAIR IN MY CLOSET! You got the black ones, but I took an inclination for the dark brown ones, bro. Yeah man, we both got good taste! You clean, you clean. I'll give you that! But I still don't know you.

"Look at him, Bluff. He ain't that smooth. Like we are going to hand over our corner to him like we're some suckas or something. Nah, bruh! It don't work like that around here."

"Man, Ace, stop trippin' on this dude," Bluff said with that same sneak-diss smile on his face. "Give the man a chance. He's probably here to get him some liquor and then go on about his business. You are getting all worked up for nothing. At least see what he is on before you form an opinion, bro. Just give him a chance. You have always jumped to conclusions about people before you give them a chance."

"Nah, bro. This ain't that. I see this fool, Bluff! Walking through the crowd all authoritatively like, flexing his muscles and sucking his teeth. Plus, you know, I can read people. Not one time have I been wrong when making a call like this. I am always right about this kind of stuff. You know it, too. Name one time I've been wrong."

"Bro, are we really doing this? Really?"

"Yup. We really IS bro, because you bogus for this."

"Ok. I'll give it to you. Ace, you are usually right about these things. But your mother, bro... you wrong about her. And you have had 18 years to see what we have seen from day one, bro. You wrong... What?! What?! Are you quiet now? I don't hear nothing!" Bluff was laughing at me again.

"Bro, gon' somewhere with that. I am not talking about my moms right now, and I am not wrong about her either! She's bogus for not being honest about my dad. I know her, bro. I know when she is lying to me. And besides, I'm not talking about my mom. I'm talking about that clown! Look at him, still trying to flex and intimidate somebody."

"Ace! Bro! You trippin'. This cat is not sucking his teeth and flexing. That's you, bro. You are the only one out here that's got all that air in your chest, man. Calm all that down, bro!" Bluff looked at me and started laughing again. "Man, you've been jumping to conclusions about people for as long as I can remember."

"Ok, Bluff. Whatever you say, man."

"GOOD! It's what I say! And I say, YOU TRIPPIN' BRO! AND I LOVE YOUR MOM, MAN. And it's time for you to stop with all this nonsense about her. I'm just saying..."

"Say what you want to say, Bluff, man. I don't care. And look at that old fool. He is flexing and sucking his teeth. I'll go over there and knock all them rotten joints right out of them black gums, old chump. Trying to make a grand entrance. Get off the stage, fool. You ain't in show bidness. This is a street corner. A streeeeet cornerrrrr, partna! My corner, fool. Show some respect when you come into another man's territory, bruh."

Bluff couldn't do anything but crack up laughing. "Brooooo! Aceee! Chill, man. What's up with you and this guy?" Bluff thought my reaction was funny and over the top. All he did was look at me laughing and shaking his head. "Ace, you need to chill out, man. Talking about the man's teeth. You betta watch out before he comes over here and knock all of your teeth out of your Grand Canyon head. It looks like you don't want none, Ace." Bluff said laughing and trying to egg me on.

"Stop playing bro, before I snatch that fool's whole grill out of his mouf." I glanced back at the old man. Our eyes met. Mine were surmising; his were slick as a gallon of 20,000-mile extended performance motor oil.

We looked each other up and down. I could feel him, and he could feel me.

I gave him a head nod.

He nodded back slightly and said, "It's all slow motion. What's up, lil' homie?" Then he walked into the liquor store.

"Oh yeah, this guy is on something," I whispered to Bluff.

"Ok, I feel you, bro. But I'm not judging the man," Bluff whispered back inconspicuously. "And yeah, he is a lil' too smooth for my taste, too. But ay, let's not judge him. Let's see how it's going to play out. Everybody comes to Bello Heights sooner or later, bro, for one thing or another. You know that. But that don't mean nothing. Look at us. We're down here just kickin' it. We got love for the corner. Let's see if he hangs around. See what his angle is…"

"Yeah, you right, Bluff, bet."

"I know I'm right, bro, but it's all good, I got you. And dude is clean, too. My man's waves are on point."

"Man, I ain't thinking about that clown, with his ashy knuckles and all those buckshots up there in his head. Those ain't no waves. Those are naps waving goodbye."

Bluff laughed so hard. "Bro!!!, you are killing me right now."

I laughed, too.

"Nah, bro. Who does he think he is? *Coming To America?* Looking like Arsenio Hall telling that girl he was the prince. Holding up that long finger and putting it on those big soup coolers, talking about, 'Shhhh, you mustn't tell a soul!' Bruh! This ain't no silent movie! YOU AT THE LIQUOR STORE, BRUH!" We laughed again.

"Ace, you a funny dude, man. You trippin', bro," Bluff said, laughing. "You are really getting fired up over this guy. You don't even know him."

"I may not know him personally, but I know his kind. I've seen dudes like him all my life, and I don't like him. Pretty punk. All shiny, and for what?"

"AAAAcccceee, calm down, bro. What's up? You are all shiny too, bro. Look at you: you've got lotion on your face and hands. Your ashy knuckles are all Jergens lotiony and thangs. You're out here with your $2 cologne splashed on your lil' dirty neck just like that clown! He probably didn't wash his neck either."

"Whatever, man. I paid over $100 for this cologne. Better recognize, bro. I don't wear nothing cheap. And how you gon' talk about my neck with that big ring around your collar, bro?"

"Ok, Mr. 'I don't wear nothing cheap...' What about these cheap jabs you keep taking at my man?"

I laugh. "You right. We are trippin', but I am telling you bro, I got a vibe about him. Game know game, bro. I don't trust this fool. I don't like him, AT ALL! He's not coming around here for nothing. These cats are not the type of guys he runs with. This dude, man, definitely has an agenda. And we gotta find out what it is."

"Wait a minute, bro... WEEEE? Ain't no WE out here. It ain't no 'we trippin'! That's all you, bro. YOU are the only one out here trippin', bro! I'm not thinking about that guy, man. I'm trying to enjoy the little time I have left and take some of these stories back home to Angel, bro. You are out here doing enough trippin' for both of us," Bluff said, laughing.

I ignored Bluff, but I still had my eye on that old cat. He stood out in the crowd because he was tall. He looked like a high-rise building in a neighborhood with

nothing but one and two-story houses and small storefronts.

Man, this dude is a mountain. He's got to be at least 6'4" or 6'5. I'm 6'1, and Bluff is 6'3", and he is taller than us both. But once I chop this fool's ego down, he will be two feet tall and shrinking.

He was strong looking for his age. Most of the guys that hung around here looked lethargic, but not him. He was stout like a bulldog and could pass for someone who may have called the shots once upon a time in his day. Maybe he was a muscle on the inside and even put in some work. He could pass for a trainer.

I folded my arms and felt my biceps. I flexed them a few times and then looked down at them.

Yeah, this dude thinks he's something.

I continued flexing my muscles, gauging whether or not I could fade this old cat if it came to that.

Man, that's a big dude. But he's old, though. He probably doesn't have the strength and speed like me. Yeah, I will wear that punk out. His day is coming...

"Listen, Bluff, I remember one of these cats really did spit some true game. He wasn't like this nickel-slick cat. He kept it 100. It was a couple of years ago, right after you left, but I'll never forget it. He was telling a story about a friend of his who used to do his girl real dirty until she got tired and put him out. I'll never forget that story...

Do what you gotta do to get the upper hand. This game ain't no joke. If you get caught sleeping, you will get squashed. You gotta have courage in this game to keep up and not get swallowed up. The game will eat you alive...

144

The lies;
The deceit;
Taking advantage of the innocent,
And having no regrets,
It's just a game,
But the damage done is real.
You gotta play on the opponent's weaknesses.
You gotta do that.
You gotta conquer and divide.
Put what they value in danger.
When you do that, your fortune can change in the
blink of an eye,
And that's the nature of this beast.
The rain and sunrays fall on the best of them, and
the worst of them,
but the lean times always lead into prosperous
times.
The great migration will soon come...
A marriage will fail.
A woman will run from her abusive boyfriend.
A family will be evicted.
A child will run away from foster care.
Emotionally distraught and mentally ill ones are
easy targets,
But anyone of those scenarios can be your next
meal.
You will eat soon,
But there is always that one -
That one that will make a difference
that one that stands out in the crowd.

*Each new dawn brings fresh new conflict. The
vultures are always watching and waiting.
Yeah, change was definitely right around the
corner. It came for him sooner than later. As I said, his girl
put him out... He got drunk one night, fell asleep on a park
bench and slept through a heavy rain. He woke up with
pneumonia. He died two weeks later. Yeah, the vultures
got him.*

That was the story...

"Nah, Bluff. We trippin' for nothing. This punk
ain't no killer."

Bluff laughed at me again.

"Nah, I'm telling you, bro, ain't nobody
intimidated by this fool. He's the type my mans described
in the story. All this punk has ever done was bully a bunch
of women and children, bro. He ain't no real G. He won't
step to no real men like us, Bluff...

Have a seat, fool, and brush them fake waves you
got on your bald head, bruh. At least my waves are all
natural. Ole sucka."

Bluff just kept laughing.

I tried to let it go, like Bluff said, but I couldn't. I
could tell he was a grimy dude... fresh on the outside but
reeking like a rotten potato on the inside. Life is nothing
but a big gym for him where he gets a workout, and all
the people that cross his path are nothing more than a
towel he hangs around his neck to wipe the sweat from
his old fuzzy eyebrows. And judging by the jailhouse
tattoos and how bulky he is, it is obvious to me that he
has not been out long. The keloids on the side of his face

and the two on his arm tell me that he's been in a few scrapes, mostly on the inside... won some, probably won them all.

What is he in there buying? What does he drink?

He emerged from the liquor store with a bottle of Schlitz Malt Liquor in his left hand and an unlit Cherry Pipe Black & Mild in his right.

He walked up to one of the old cats and put the Cherry Pipe Black & Mild in his mouth. The old man didn't wait for him to ask for a light. I could see his poor drunk hands trembling ever so slightly as he tried to light the fat, cherry smelling cigar without shaking.

The energy on the corner changed the minute this fool walked on the scene. All of the laughter and storytelling ceased. All eyes were now fixed on him. I had to admit that I wish I had that kind of power, that all I had to do is walk up on a scene and get respect just by my presence. That's real muscle. I get it in my organization but can't get it on the street from a bunch of drunks... it makes me wonder... what's this guy got that I don't have.

After 10 or 15 minutes of polite, personal exchanges between individuals, the newcomer's spell was broken when one wino started laughing loudly and telling the other drunk to stop lying. It was infectious. Everyone joined in, and the festivities were back on. They went around in circles telling tall tales of how they saved the world, escaped the jaws of death, beat an entire mob of angry black people when they were sick and recovering from the flu!

"See, Bluff, I told you these cats are full of hot air, man, but they are wild. I love coming down here, man."

We laughed hysterically.

"Yeah, true, true. But I'm telling you, Ace, bro, most of what they say has some element of truth to it. Sometimes I think they confess in these stories. They mix it up with exaggeration and watery white lies, but the truth is speckled in there somewhere. Some of these guys have done some terrible things and haven't told a soul. Instead of holding it in, they let it out here in their own creative ways. At least that's my take on the things they say."

"Yeah, I can see that."

14

NEW GUY

We hung around with the old cats at the liquor store for hours, chewing the fat.

During this time, we found out that the cat that lit the new guy's Black & Mild told him about this spot. They did some time together, a good spell back in the day. He just did a dime for some repeat offender stuff, robbing, breaking and entering, etc. So now that he is out and does not have any real place to go, he's stopping through here. As old as he is, he needs to chill out with all that breaking and entering and get a real job.

"Man Ace, I miss this scene. These are some good dudes, you know. They are a little misguided, that's all. Maybe I can make a difference for some of them, you know, drop some of my young-man knowledge on them."

I looked at Bluff and just smiled. "Maybe man, who knows. I know your tongue is just as slick as theirs."

We both started laughing again.

"Look at that dude, Bluff. He ain't nothing but a Laurence Fishburne wanna-be. I'll go over there and slap that Black & Mild out of that fool's mouth. Then I'll drink his beer. Listen to him bragging. Ain't nothing he saying is facts. My lying momma got more facts than him, bro. Look at him."

"Dude, lay off your mother. And I know you know, I feel like she's my momma too, bro. We just had this conversation on the way up here, an hour ago, 10 minutes ago, and now! Chill with all that, bro!"

I moved a few steps closer toward the crowd but tried to be slick about it. The new cat keyed in but turned his head slightly so he would not reveal that he peeped my move. I thought that was pretty cool. I smiled to myself.

Ok, you've got a lil' style about you. I'll give you that.

Then the opportunity opened, and he had a chance to speak...

"Yeah, you young cats can learn something from a real playa' like myself. I have made a lot of mistakes in life, but I've had my share of successes too, if you know what I mean. I know I am new out here, and you cats don't know me. And I don't plan on being here long. I just stopped through to see my man. We met back in the day, but I'd like to say something before I make my next move."

Like all the other old heads, he was looking at me and Bluff and the other young cats standing around drinking, smoking, and wasting time on the corner with them. He winked at us, and the older cats burst into laughter. So did we.

I think we chose this corner because of moments like this... *Man, that was pretty slick too. Ok, I'll give him that one as well, but he will have to earn the rest of them.*

The old cat spoke, "The secret to life, youngbloods, is don't get caught. See, when you are young and thirsty like I was, you get caught. I was a hothead, out there burglarizing, carjacking, breaking and entering, and even putting in real work from time to time. You young cats know what I mean, but I wasn't thinking. And to make it out here, you gotta use your head. The one up here, if you know what I mean." He was tapping the side of his temple.

Our eyes locked again. It was like I knew where he was going. The only thing I kept wondering, though, is '*where have I seen this guy before?*' *Why does he seem familiar? I know this cat. Does he know me? Is he an undercover cop? Does he know what I do? This fool bet not be no narc!*

My guards went up again. I continued listening to every word his nickel-slick tongue spilled out, but he wasn't fooling me. Game recognizes game.

I know this fool is going to slip up and give away his cover. Yeah, keep talking, fool.

The old cat continued, "Another thing young cats need to know is how to deal with these women out here, if you know what I mean. I used to check them, but only when I had to. But you know how that goes.

"Yeah, like this one girl, her name was Champagne – not Sherry, not Shannon. Her name was Champagne. She was the only girl I knew with that name. And that's why I made her mine. And she knew how to work it. She knew how to let it roll off her tongue. She was classy, too, just like Champagne. Plus, she was fine as can be. She carried herself like a fine glass of champagne. She enjoyed being spoiled. So, I bought her nice things, and kept her hair and nails done. But Champagne talked too much, and that's the one thing that a woman can do to piss me all the way off. She didn't know how to keep her mouth closed. She was a show-off. Always talking about what I did for her and how I spoiled her.

"And you see, it was right there where she messed up, but I didn't catch it at first. I let that slip by me. I was young in the game, though. I made a few slip-ups here and there, but I never made the same one twice. That's some playa' wisdom that I just dropped on you. Live by that. Never make the same mistake twice, and some mistakes, never make at all. I wasn't hip to game when I got started but I learned quickly."

He glanced at me again for a quick second.

I nodded with a straight face, but in my mind, I was saying, *"You already know, playa'."*

"Anyway, back to the story. See, Champagne thought I was her man, but she learned the hard way that I was never her man. She was just one of my side chicks. She got twisted up in the game because I bought her a few things. She let that fur coat get in her head, but my guy gave me that coat. It didn't cost me a dime. I got with her on a regular, because the girl was definitely talented, if you know what I mean."

Everyone started laughing.

"But that was my business. Champagne seemed to think it was her business and that she could tell it. So, she was always opening her mouth about how I bought her an expensive fur coat. But, on another tip, what else was a playa' of my reputation supposed to do. Fur coats, watches, jewelry, purses, clothes, and shoes... that's just what I did back in the day. Money and mathematics were my thang, young playas'. Materialistic gain was never an issue for me.

"I want you young cats to hear me when I say that. Things came to me easily. I had skills. I knew how to get what I needed. Cars, women, tricks, hoes. All of it came with the game.

"But as I said, Champagne kept talking. And one night, she did not know that my lady was in the club listening to her shoot off her fat mouth about how good I was to her, calling my name out and everything.

"That's some more playa' knowledge. A playa' can have many hoes, but he ain't got but one woman. And he will check her, but he can also trust her.

"Well, I guess you know the end of that story, but don't trip. I handled it. I checked my woman for questioning me about what she heard some broad say in a nightclub, and of course, I cut Champagne off like a hangnail. But in true playa' style, I got another Champagne that same night. They came a dime a dozen back in the day, and I took the fur coat and gave it to the next side chick. That's some more game. A true playa' don't waste nothing. My new side chick was just as happy to don that fur as the old Champagne. And I promise you, the old one knows how to keep her fat mouth shut now."

The crowd was mesmerized. You could hear side conversations breaking out, people saying how cold he was and what a playa' move that was. Even I was a little impressed with it.

Ok, my mans handled that situation, but that was back in his day. These girls don't listen to dudes like that these days. I'd like to know how he would handle one of these girls. See what kind of pointers he has.

I wanted to ask him that question, but I didn't want him to think that he was schooling me like he was my daddy or something. So, I said nothing and just kept listening in the background. Our eyes continued to meet off and on.

154

He took a quick break and went back into the store and came out with a six-pack. He pulled one from the pack and placed the rest in one of the ice chests and sat on top of it.

By this time, other guys had stepped up and were telling their war stories.

One of the guys talked about how he used to have trouble with his women back in the day because he used to run the streets a lot. He was a hothead back then who loved to gamble and would often spend a lot of his time trying to gain back the money he lost. He ended up spending time in jail for running checks and a credit card scam. He went on and on. So did a few others. But I couldn't wait to hear more from the new cat. He had my ear. I was intrigued. The more he talked, the more I wanted to hear what he had to say.

He finally got the floor back.

"Yeah, you see. Let me finish hollering at you young cats. The game has changed in many aspects, but it's the same in the most important ways. And if you don't remember nothing else, always remember this: it's your world, homie."

I got it. I understood what he was saying. It was up to me to create my vision in life. *Man...* I thought to myself. *This guy is deep.*

"And to show you what I mean," he said. "Listen to this...

"I know this cat from back in the day. He was a known killer, real tough guy. Even the toughest guys in the neighborhood were intimidated around him. This guy would do anything. He would start fights, wreck house parties and crash gambling parties. We were at this one party, and this cat came in and looked around the room. Out of nowhere, he picked up a bottle, broke it and stabbed the owner of the house in the face. He told everybody that it was his party now, and that he was the houseman. Being the houseman meant he got a big cut of everybody's winnings, and that was that. He was known for that kind of behavior. And no one left the party because they were afraid of the backlash.

"But that wasn't the worst of that night. When all the gambling, drinking, and partying was over, he followed one young lady home and forced his way into her house. Word on the street was he raped her and moved into her house that night. We saw him coming in and out like his name was on the lease, like he paid the rent. She became his woman, and that was that. There was nothing she could do about it. Everybody in the neighborhood was shocked but was too afraid to say anything. Eventually he went to jail, and that's how she got out of the prison he had her in."

Bluff and I looked at one another.

"If it was me," I said to Bluff, "I would have destroyed that dude. I would have had to step up, man. There's no way I would let anybody do my sister like that, or even any of my nieces. Ain't no way."

"Yeah, Ace. I know what you mean. Hearing that story was rough. I couldn't have let that one slide either."

I looked at the guy and, to my surprise, he was already staring at me.

"That was foul, youngblood. A real playa' is also a gentleman. He doesn't have to take a woman by force. If he treats her well and makes her feel like she is the only woman in the world, she will invite him to her home, playa'. That's some more playa' knowledge for you."

And like that, I was back in, all ears...

"As I said earlier, I was a playa'. I did a little gambling and some roughhousing but being a playa' was my thang. And one thang that the women I dealt with knew was that if they got out of line, I would put them back in line... even if it meant I had to slap the taste out of their mouth.

"I wasn't like this cat that I just told you about. I didn't have to strongarm my way into anybody's house or nothing like that. That wasn't a smart move. What if I walked up in there and she had a man in there, or she lived with her brothers or uncle or parents or something? So those kinds of moves are not always smart, and they can backfire on you.

"So, I had my own way with the women, and the women respected the game. And this is how the game went back in the day...

"When a woman got out of pocket, if she was your woman, you had to put her back in pocket. And as a playa', you tried to be smooth about it. But sometimes, they would try you and start talking slick and disrespectful. That's when you might have to get a little physical, because, under no circumstances, can a woman be allowed to disrespect a playa'. That's a cardinal rule in the Playa's Handbook."

Bluff and I looked at one another again and shook our heads.

"That's what I was telling you about Shaquita," I said to Bluff. "That girl always had something to say. That's why I am not with her. She needs to go on and finish college and get with one of those white-collar, obedient dudes from Harvard or somewhere, because I will slap the taste out of her mouth."

"Ace," Bluff said, "You are crazy, man. You are not going to put your hands on that girl." We laughed and continued listening to the story.

The old cat continued, "...I remember this one chick walked up on me while I was standing around talking with some other playas'. Man, she wasn't even that cute. I don't even remember her name. She was angry because I hadn't seen her in about four or five days, but she heard that I was right around the corner from her house. She walked up on me and tried to check me in front of my guys. She pushed me in my chest, and put her finger in my face. I looked at my guys; they had gotten quiet, waiting to see how I would respond. She told me to never come around her neighborhood and not to come to her house to see her.

"At that moment, I tried to slap all the teeth out her mouth. Unfortunately, only one of them hit the ground.

"I understood that she wanted to spend time with a playa' like myself, but that is no excuse to walk up on me, talking crazy and fronting me off. See, that's what I am trying to get you youngbloods to understand, these women need to be schooled. She learned her lesson, and I felt good about my contribution to her training."

Everybody in the crowd was in awe of the new guy. He was so smooth, I wanted to go upside his head because ain't nobody smooth as me. But I had to give it to him; he was laying down some real game. So, I didn't trip. I kept listening.

"But, in all fairness, when it comes to violence, you have to be careful because you can get caught up. I remember this one girl. She was beautiful. I loved this girl. She was fine as can be… finer than my girl Champagne. She was short and very petite, but she was stacked up nicely, you know, thicker than a Snicker."

You could see lightbulbs going off in the minds of all the dirty old men in the crowd. Hey, even Bluff and I had a few lights flickering in our minds.

"She had them baby-making hips and that big old thang wagging behind her. Man, this girl… oooweee. A playa' couldn't get enough."

I whispered to Bluff, "This fool lying. Ain't no girl that fine giving him the time of day. He describing Beyonce or somebody. This fool lying, bro," Bluff just laughed at me.

He continued, "She had the biggest, prettiest eyes and the cutest smile. Man, I loved her smile. It was like all the white keys on the piano would strum one by one when she flashed those pearly whites at me, youngbloods. She had naturally long, pretty hair too, but cut it. She didn't bother to get all those wig extensions or whatever young ladies call them these days. She was all-natural, but it didn't make a difference; short hair or long,

she was still fine as can be. I liked it long, and so did she,
IF YOU KNOW WHAT I MEAN.

Everyone started laughing.

"But the short hair was cool. It was a nice
compliment to her sassy attitude. I'm telling y'all
youngbloods, this girl was special. She had a beautiful
mind and a beautiful spirit, and it was all wrapped in a
perfectly golden-bronze melanin package. Man, I can see
this girl in my mind right now. I should have never let her
get away. What was that girl's name...? Well, I can't think
of it right now, but it will come to me in a minute."

I could hear those old cats in the background
saying that they would have loved to have had a girl as
fine as her and that they wished they could have seen her
when he was dating her. I was thinking the same thing. I
would have wanted to see a girl that fine.

"Yeah, youngbloods, she was the most beautiful
girl I have ever laid eyes upon, from that day to this day.
And the first time I saw her, I made up in my mind that I
had to have her.

"The first time my eyes fell on her, I was sitting
outside on my front porch, playing cards and kickin' it
with my guys. The bus stop was only a block away at the
end of the corner. When she stepped off the bus, I saw
her from the corner under the street light. I couldn't make
out her facial features, but that shape, maannn... that's all
I needed to see! She was hitting it on every shadow. I've
never seen a more curvaceous woman in all my life. I
started sitting on the porch every night after that. She had
to walk passed my spot to make it to hers, just a block or
two away. One of my guys knew her family. They were

good people, he said. She had a little job or something after school, and I used to sit out there on the porch just so I could get her attention.

I used to sing songs when she walked past. I'd hit her with "Just My Imagination," by The Temptations, Stevie Wonder's "Isn't She Lovely," and The Isley Brothers' "Who's That Lady."

"Because I was a good dancer, sometimes I would stand up and put some of my Temptations moves on her.

At first, she would never smile, but I knew I was breaking her down. At times, she would look my way but turn her head quickly, jerking her little neck and everything, the way girls do when they are attracted to a playa' such as myself, but are trying to play hard to get. I knew I had her though, because I never went after one and didn't get her. My mouthpiece with the women is just like that. They can't tell me no. Eventually, I get them all. And I still got it, youngbloods. Don't let this salt and pepper mustache fool you. I have a hot lil' tenderoni on my radar right now. It won't be long. I'll have her eating out of my hands in no time.

"But the more I said things like 'Hey cutie,' 'Hey beautiful,' and continued singing those Motown hits to her, I could see her defenses dropping every single day. Sometimes I'd look in the mirror and just smile at myself and wonder how I got so smooth. She started dressing more provocatively and started wearing her hair in curls or something. All I knew is that she was as fine as can be.

So, one day as she got off the bus stop and was coming down the street, I got off the porch and asked her

if she would take a little time to talk to me. And unlike before, she said, 'Yes.'

"Maaan. Let me tell y'all young cats something. I laid some of the coldest and slickest game a playa' can lay, and before I knew it, she was mine. I moved her in with me right away, but, of course, that was a big mistake. Because after a time, I saw who she was, and she saw who I was.

"She was a sweet woman, and I really admired that about her. I enjoyed being in her presence. But that didn't change the fact that I was true to the game. She was trying to turn my facts into her fiction. She struggled with the facts and refused to accept the obvious... that she was number one but would never be the only one. Hear me youngbloods. That's some real playa' insight right there. Facts.

"I treated her like a queen when we were at home or when we were out together, but like the playa' that I was, when I was in the street, I did what playas' do, feel me, youngbloods?

"The problem was, I loved her. And deep down inside, I somehow felt she had earned the right to want, and to even try, to change me and try to convince me to grow up and be a better person. She even had the courage to tell me that with the life that I was living, I was going nowhere fast, and that it was time for me to grow up and mature more as a man to continue being with her.

"I knew she was right, but for some reason, that made me very angry.

"A playa' wasn't a playa' if he didn't have his cake and eat it too. She was trying to strip me down. But a playa' will never land on a stripper's pole. He will always land on his feet. Always. She didn't understand that I was a true playa', and that no woman, under no circumstances, at no time of day or night, and no matter how beautiful, flawless, and fine she was... she was still not allowed to talk when she had been given instructions to hold her peace.

"Who did she think she was that she could talk to me that way? Like she had the authority to call me out. This was one of those cases where I had to check her. My old character stood up in the raw, wearing a wife beater and sweatpants, ready to put in work.

"And since I am keeping it 100 with you youngbloods, I must say that she wasn't coming at me reckless at all. I was just in my feelings and didn't want to look in that mirror of truth. See, a playa' has the right to be in his feelings from time to time. I mean, you know... my world, my money, my rules. So, I tried to stay in character. I tried to be a playa' with her. So, I shut her down, and I was nice about it. I simply told her to shut her mouth, and to shut up talking to me. You know, some dumb playa' stuff like that. Y'all know how we do when we wrong and don't want to admit it. We go all *Silence of the Lambs* on them. Tell them to shut up talking to us and to get out of our faces."

I smiled because I used to do Shaquita that way. I know I was bogus, but she was always on me about hustling, just like his girl was on him about being a playa'.

"You see, youngbloods, she was falling hard for me and really wanted us to have a future together. I had fallen for her too, but I wasn't about to change. Neither was she, with her feisty behind. I mean, this little pint-sized woman had a mouth the size of an alligator. I'm not referring to it being big or loud. It was her words. They would crush me. I had no defense against them. I can't recall one time where she was wrong, when she was checking me on my mess.

"Maaan, that girl was always right. I loved it, but I hated it at the same time. As a matter of fact, she was the only girl that ever made me even think about changing.

"And to be honest with you young cats, that's good for a playa'. If you find a woman who will keep it 100 with you, and you know she loves you and has your best interest in mind... she's the one, youngstas. She's a keeper. Don't let that one go. Keep her close to your heart, and don't take her for granted. Take it from a real playa'. I'm telling you what I know, not what I heard.

"Well, as I was saying... She wouldn't let up. She kept nagging me about changing and becoming something else other than a playa'. And see, that's another lesson that is hard for these females to learn. Me personally, I don't get it. Shut up talking, end of lesson. That's it, that's all. It ain't no freedom of speech when a playa' says put a benchmark in it. PUT A BENCHMARK IN IT, WOMAN! That's simple arithmetic if you ask me. They have got to learn that they can't change a grown man, and talking to him like he's a boy will not end well for them. It only ignites an already volatile situation and puts more fuel on the flames. It's a recipe for disaster, and she is the one that will get burned to a crisp. How many times does a broad need to be taught that lesson? I think all females know that when a man speaks, that's law. I believe they go toe to toe because of the makeup sex. I'm just saying. She knows that if she talks back, I am going to slap the taste out of her mouth. She goes somewhere and pouts for a minute. I'll go out and do my thang. And when I return, she is all on a playa'. So, what else could it be other than the makeup sex?

"I'm serious, youngbloods. She used to challenge me about changing all the time. And this one particular day, I really wasn't in the mood to hear her flapping her gums. I was generous all that week-long by letting her get it off her chest... and it was cute for a minute. But when I say chill, it's time to chill. By the weekend, she was still at it. I was trying to set the evening mood, enjoy her walking around the house in one of my t-shirts, help her with the laundry, drink a little wine, eat some shrimp scampi. You know, enjoy a very leisurely day with my woman. Get a little frisky with her. Put something heavy on her mind. Have a deep conversation with her. Take her to a whole new level all day long before I go out and engage the nightlife. She was cramping my style. I asked her to back off, but she dug in deeper. And before I knew it, I had slapped her down to the living room floor like she was one of them hoes out there on the corner of 69th and Lubric. But that was my bad. I should have never let a female pull me out of playa' mode and put me into pimp mode.

"But nonetheless, that was on me. I watched in terror and shame as her head hit the corner of that glass coffee table. But what was I supposed to do? I had to teach her a lesson: leave a playa' be when he's not trying to be bothered.

"She screamed on the way down, and all I could do is jack up my pants and walk out the door. I left her right there on the floor, in her own blood and shattered shards of glass. I went out that night and had a good time, like a playa' should have. I was letting her know that I could care less about how fine she was or the fact that I made her my woman. A female can never be allowed to step to a playa'. Never. That's a lesson that all broads have to be taught, one way or another. It was a hard lesson, the hardest I've ever taught, but she learned. Her face was ruined after that. She was carved from her eyebrow to her chin, and then some.

"I'm telling you young cats this, because I went too far. She was young, man. She was a petite woman, too. I regretted that entire situation, but I mean, I tried to tell her to leave me alone. But she kept ragging a brother, you know what I mean? I lost my temper and snapped. But I really didn't mean for it to go that far. It wasn't my intention to hurt her.

"When I came back home, she had gotten up from the floor but left the broken glass right there on the floor, marinating in her blood. I called one of my partners over to the crib, and he patched her up. He gave her a few bootleg stitches, you know. That way the altercation was clean. No need to get the cops involved in a playa's bidness, right? But like I said, she was the most beautiful woman I had ever laid eyes on, at least before she messed up her face, and for what? All because she couldn't keep her fat mouth shut. But one thing I can say, she sure was loyal and loved me. But, like all my ladies, she couldn't help herself. After that blow to her face, we started

166

fighting all the time. I felt a lil' sorry for her because I no longer looked at her the same. I hate it when a woman lets herself go. That scar went clean up and down her face too, man. Wasn't nothing she could do about that.

"Man, youngbloods, I can't remember her name. What was that girl's name?"

NEW

Momma

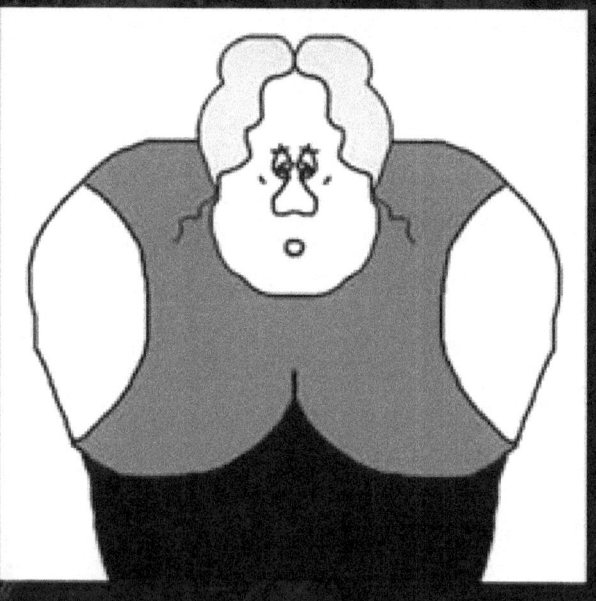

Bluff elbowed me and nodded his head with an astounded look on his face. I looked in the direction of his nod. All I saw was a short, stubby lumberjack of sorts... or maybe a woman who was not only having a bad day but was having a bad LIFE. I am not sure what he/she/it is/was/wants to be/could have been/should have been... I WAS CONFUSED! I'll put it like this, it looked like an orangutan clad as a woman or a whole circus act passing through the infamous Bello Heights. I really couldn't distinguish exactly what it was that I saw trundling in our direction.

"Woah! What's up, Bluff? C'mon man, why are you bothering that woman? Does it look like she needs another joke cracked on her? Well, allow me! She CLEARLY has issues. Look at her face! She looks like she had coals of fire and industrial-sized hammers thrown at her and her face caught every one! This lady looks like she's been chewing on cinder blocks! I bet she's been eating bowls of gravel for breakfast with spoiled milk! Her teeth are so yellow, she makes the sun jealous! Whewwww! She smells like a dumpster on garbage day! And look at them big ole jowls... she looks like she's hoarding buried treasure in her face! Aaahh! Crazy!

"And now, Bluff, here you are, adding more insult to her unfortunate injury. Leave that woman be, man. It looks like she's still hungry and ready to chew you up, then use your bones to pick the meat out of her teeth to cap off her afternoon snack. Don't bother that circus act. Just let it pass by. Be polite, wave softly, and keep your head down. Just don't give it eye contact. Eye contact may be a trigger."

"Ace, you are hilarious. That's my dad's girlfriend, my 'new Momma.' That's the one I told you about that he introduced me to."

"Whaaat?! Wordddd?!"

"Yeah, man, that's her."

Bluff waited for my response.

STILL WAITING...

"Man, Bluff... HOW?! Is this real? Is she real? HOW?!"

MY HEAD DROPS AND WAGS SIDE TO SIDE... "I don't know what to say."

I'M SPEECHLESS...

I look at Bluff with confused pity and say, "Aaay, I'm sorry, Bluff, man. I'm sorry. Is your pops ok? Is he sick? Does he have a brain tumor or something? Is dementia kicking in early for him? I know this must be hard for you... but there has got to be some state-funded programs out there to help you deal with this, bruh..."

We both swallowed our humor while looking as polite as possible as she quickly approached us.

She noticed Bluff right off. Neither of us could ignore her flailing arms and loud voice ringing in our ears as she approached us. We moved a good distance from the crowd and met her in tow, to indulge her and not disrupt the boozing crowd. She hugged us both like we were longtime lovers and friends.

"So, Bluff, who's your handsome pal," she asked with her eyeballs dangling from the sockets and unwrapping me like a watermelon Jolly Rancher, while giving my cheeks a generous, openhanded rub before I mustered the strength to snatch away from the gluttonous, grappling grip that she pretended was an innocent hug.

"Hey, Momma. This is my friend, Ace. We grew up together."

"Welllll, helloooo, Ace." She was all gills and grins. Bluff and I looked at one another and sorta cleared our throats.

"Sooo, what are you two handsome fellas doing down here in Bello Heights this time of morning? It's too early to get your drink on, unless you are drinking with Momma. Y'all fellas want to drink with Momma this morning, don't ya?"

"We'd love to, but not today, Momma. But thanks for the offer. Ace and I were just hanging out reminiscing and going down memory lane. We used to hang out here as kids. Well, old Ace was a kid, but he had a good head on his shoulders, so I kicked it with him anyway. We know a lot of these cats, Momma. And what are you doing down here, Momma? Shouldn't you be at home with your man?"

"Boy don't no man runs Momma. I comes and goes as I pleases." Momma turned away from Bluff and threw her hungry fisheyes on me. "And right now, Ace, you handsome hunk of flesh, you can come and go as you pleases too. Momma's got you, baby, with your fine self, all young and strong looking."

AWKWARD... I laugh and drop my head in pure, unadulterated, virgin shame.

"Nah, Momma," I said. "I'm good, but thank you, sweetie." I could see Bluff bursting at the seams underneath his breath.

"Yeah, we are good, Momma…" Bluff said.

"Come on Bluff, let's get back to the crowd. We are missing out on the stories. Good meeting you, Momma."

"Stories?" Momma asked. "What fool is telling a story? I know all those fools. They have been doing this for years. They are not telling stories. They are telling lies. I can't believe this is what you young fellas are down here doing. I could have been showing you both a good time by now. I can't believe that y'all will turn down Momma's gud-gud for some ole wino babbling. Lord, what is this world coming to?"

We ignore Momma and start walking back toward the crowd. Momma takes it upon herself to follow us.

"Yeah, it's been a minute since I hung out down here. Ole Momma thanks y'all for letting her hang out with you. Such nice fellas, both of you.

Bluff and I looked at each other.

I smiled and said, "Absolutely, Momma, come on."

After Momma invited herself to join us, we decided to stay a few yards behind the crowd because she was excited and extremely talkative. But we could still hear the new cat, so, it was all good.

"Why are you fine, handsome, strong young men out here listening to these old drunk fools when you could be somewhere with me making magic happen." Momma looked around to see who was in the crowd. She began pointing out familiar faces. Then, like everyone else, her eyes, like a magnet, were drawn to the new guy.

Just a minute ago, she was all on me. I should call Bluff's father, tell him to come check his gilled friend. He will slap the taste out of her rachet juke joint mouth.

"...Y'all youngstas back there feel me?" The new guy said with a nod. We nodded back, although we had no idea what he was talking about. "Yeah, because, as I said, I didn't look at her the same. And even after we made up, she continued trying to change me. We'd fight, things would escalate, and then we would kiss and make up. But eventually, youngbloods, you gotta know when to cash in your chips, if you know what I mean. I ended up letting her go and moving on. She just didn't get it for me anymore. I don't know whatever came of her after I split."

"Wait a minute," Momma said. "What is this guy talking about? Who is he talking about?"

"He ain't saying nothing, Momma," I said. Bluff looked at me and started laughing.

"Oh, I see Ace. She's your momma now, hmm?" Bluff said while laughing.

Momma said, "Oh, both of you shut your face. I know him."

"Who? The guy up there talking," I asked.

"Yes. I know him, and he's a dreadful man. I got to go. I got to get away from here!" Momma turned briskly and started walking away from us like she just received an urgent phone call. We followed behind her and stopped her right away. I got in front of her and asked her to stop.

"Hold on, Momma. What's wrong. Why are you so upset?" I asked.

"I just got to go and get away from here. I don't want anything to do with that creep."

"How do you know him, Momma?"

"Look, growing up, I used to live up north in a small town just outside of the big city."

"Where? New York?"

"No, but that doesn't matter. WHY WOULD THEY LET HIM OUT OF JAIL?!!! For what he did to that girl, he should be locked under the jail, and the key should be melted down in an incinerator, right along with his foul soul!"

"Wait, waaait... what girl?" I asked. We walked away from the crowd a little further. I wanted to hear what Momma knew about this new guy without being interrupted.

"Tell us, Momma," Bluff said. "What girl?"

"I don't know. She was just a girl that I went to school with. We were not friends, nor were we in the same classes. I would see her in the halls or in the cafeteria during lunch. I remember her because I thought she was really cute. She was always in the school newsletter or yearbook for one achievement or another. I was a few years older than her. You know, they held me back a few times. But she wasn't supposed to be in high school. She was like 12 or 13 years old, maybe 14, I don't really remember. But I do know that she was really young and super smart. Almost smart as me. She was taking all senior classes, and some college courses as well. She was what they called a prodigy. But that didn't come as a surprise to anyone. She was a real brain. She graduated a couple years early. You know Ace, I could have graduated early, too, if they would have stopped playing favorites."

"I know you could have, Momma. But don't sweat it. Regardless of how they tried to hold you back, you still came out on top. Look at you, Momma. You turned out to be an intelligent and good-looking woman. You are a prize to any man, Momma. So don't sweat it. I need you to finish telling me what happened to the girl..."

"Hmmmm. So, you think ole Momma's intelligent, hmmm?" She said cheesing like Chester Cheetah.

"Yes, I do, Momma. If you were just 35 and a half years younger, you'd be swinging on my arm right now, but I'm serious, Momma. Stop playing. Tell me, what happened to the girl..."

Momma grabbed the beaded purse resting snugly between the layers of cushion in the meaty fold of her arm, unsnapped it and pulled out her private stash. In one greedy gulp, she emptied the small silver container that she filled with the spirited elixir right before coming to Bello Heights. She drank most of it on the way. The strong moonshine concoction did not phase her. She replaced the cap tightly, placed the aluminum container back into its beaded cove, stuffed the beaded sack back between her oily creases of fatty meat tissues, then looked up at the new guy angrily, pointed at him as if her finger was a bullet, then spoke her mind...

"H E   H A P P E N E D..." He destroyed that girl's life!" Momma began hyperventilating. "I got to get out of here!"

"Calm down, Momma. It's going to be ok. We got you. You are with me... Ace. I'm like a vault, Momma. You're safe. Trust. I got you. Bluff's got you. Now calm down, and take a deep breath."

"I gotta get my drank and get away from this corner. I can't be on the same planet as that guy! I moved almost six states away to get away from him! WHAT IS HE DOING HERE! JESUS! GET ME OUT OF HERE. I CAN'T BE HERE. I GOT TO GO!"

"Mommaaaaa...., c a l m   d o w n . . . Calm down, baby. Bluff and I got you." I turned to Bluff and said, "Bluff, go in there, bro, and get Momma her drink. It's on me." I turned back to Momma, "Just calm down, Momma. Bluff and I, we got you. Bluff is going to get you whatever you want." I turned to Bluff again, "Get her a six-pack, man, and whatever else she has a taste for." I looked at Momma, "What are you tasting?"

Momma's jowls begin to swell and pulse back and forth. I guess I hit her sweet spot with the drink. "Wait Bluff, forget the six-pack. Get her a case, man."

"Mmmmhmmm! Young and generous! Where were you when I was young and thirsty, Mr. Generous Man Wild Thang?"

I tried to act as if I didn't hear her, thinking she would stop with all the shenanigans.

"Don't ignore ole Momma, you young thang. You will miss out if you do. The past doesn't have to be our future, sweetie. We here NOW! It's not too late for you to be my Ace in the hole. Momma will treat you right, baby."

I smiled. "Momma stop, you play too much."

She started laughing.

"Now stop playing, what are you tasting?"

"Baby, a case is fine. Bring Momma a couple cases of Budweiser, would you, honey?"

Bluff nodded, shook his head in amusement, then proceeded toward the door.

"And get me a couple bottles of Henney too, would you, honey? I'mma need something stronger than that Budweiser. Momma's traumatized!"

Bluff looked back at me and laughed. I smiled humorously and gave him the nod.

"Anything you want, Momma. I got you. It's on me. But I need you to finish telling me about this guy. I knew this fool was foul."

"No problem, baby, anything for you, Ace. Ay, Bluff, get me a couple packs of them Swisher Sweets!" Momma said to Bluff. Ace nodded again.

"Alright, where was I, Ace??? Nevermind, shut up, I remember… The girl… All I know is that little girl graduated from high school early. She was like 14, or 12 or something. She was young and smart and really wasn't old enough to be in high school. She went to college that same school year on a full-ride scholarship deal. Ain't that something? She was on a scholarship at 12 or 13 years old, and there I was 20 going on 21, and I was still stuck there at that dumb school. I'm smart, but everybody wanted to treat me like I wasn't anything. But I have always been special. Just ask my granny, Nana. She will tell you. You should have seen me in science class. I could…"

"I know, Momma, and I am not trying to cut you off," I said. "I know you were smart in school. You are still smart now, and beautiful. You are smart and beautiful, Momma. But let's get back to how you know this guy."

"All I know is that she went to college and was gone for a whole year. After her freshman year in college, she came back to town for the summer. She had gotten a job at the mall just so she wouldn't be bored. She'd catch the bus to and from work. This clown used to lurk, watching the girls. The younger they were, the more his brain got gassed up and perverted. Well, to make a long story short, he started plotting in his mind how he was going to trap her. He tried to talk to her, but she wouldn't give him the time of day. Her mind was on college and enjoying the summer with family and friends... WHAT'S TAKING BLUFF SO LONG?! The line is never around the corner. I got to get back to my Boo Thang!"

"Momma, stay focused. THE GIRL... What happened with the girl? He started plotting against her, then what?"

"Then he jacked her up."

"Jacked her up? What did he do? Did he kill her?"

"No, but he may as well had killed her. Her life was over after that. Is Bluff on the way? I needs my drank."

"He'll be out in a minute. How did he jack her up? Why was her life over after that?"

"He tried to kill her, but she lived. It was all on the news and everything... *FEMALE 15-YEAR-OLD COLLEGE STUDENT ATTACKED IN ALLEY AND LEFT FOR DEAD...*

I looked up at dude, and he was staring at me again. This time my eyes were cold as steel. He didn't seem shaken. He gave me another nod. He was totally clueless to what I was learning about him, as clueless as that little girl was.

178

"What else, Momma? I need you to tell me everything!"

"As I said, he jacked that poor girl up. He used to sit out on his porch and harass her when she would get off the bus. He'd say nasty things to her. Things that would turn even a girl like me off. And as you can see, Momma's never turned off... Maybe we can leave here and drink this Henney together."

I smiled slightly. "Momma you are a trip, but as you said, maybe another day and time, if you were just a few years younger. Finish telling me about this girl."

"Yeah, like I said, he would harass her when she got off the bus and walk pass his house to get home. It had gotten so vulgar that she started crossing to the other side of the street to avoid them, but it didn't help. He got louder and louder with his obscenities. But she didn't worry much, because she thought he was just a drunken fool. And he never tried to leave the porch and follow her or anything like that. It was just him and a few other guys on the porch messing with people as they passed by. The other guys would just laugh and then tell her things like 'get home safe, baby', Stuff like that. But the dreadful man you see up there talking right now, it wasn't a game for him. No sirrrr. He was a low-life, for sure."

"Ok. Break that down for me, Momma. Don't leave anything out. Tell me everything," I said while looking directly at him.

"Well, one night, she got off the bus, crossed the street, and it was just the two friendlier guys on the porch. They spoke and told her to get home safely, like they always did. Once she got past their house, she crossed back to the other side of the street and was continuing to the next block, where she lives.

"When she got to the alley, before she could scream, he had already grabbed her, put his hand over her mouth, and dragged her into the alley where his car, duct tape, and ropes were waiting... he said to her, 'One word, and you are dead. I will snap your neck like a twig from a tree and won't lose any sleep. Now try me. Get in there and sit down and don't move.'"

Bluff finally arrived with Momma's Hennessy, two cases of Budweiser, and some Swishers.

"About time. Open that for me, baby. Momma done worked up a thirst."

Bluff proceeded to reach down to open one of the cases of beer.

"No, no, Bluff, don't patronize Momma this morning. Just screw that top off that bottle of Henney. Beer ain't gon' do it for me right now." She drank a quarter bottle before coming up for air.

BURRRRRRP!!!

"Man! Love me some Henney. You fellas want a swig?"

"No thank you," I said.

"So, where were we?" Oh, yeah, we were about to get this party started."

"Momma, no. Stop," I said. "Get back to the story."

"Ok. Ok, handsome. Momma's just fiddling with you. Soooo, anyway, he drives toward a vacant building, a good way from the alley where they live, about 25 miles away, in a deserted part of a rundown side of town. When they finally stopped at a red light, she went for the door handle so that she could open the door and jump out. He laughed and said,

See, I know how girls like you think. All uppity, thinking you smarter than me. Well, you ain't, and now I'm going to teach your stuck-up tail another lesson. All girls like you need to be taught and trained. Always making men feel like scum bags. Well, who's the scum bag now?

She started crying. That's when he backhanded her.

I told you not to say a word! All that crying is included!

His ring left a cut in her face just above her eye. The tears and blood mingling together impaired her vision.

Yeah, I took all the door handles off. To get out of here, you have to climb over me, but don't worry; you are going to be climbing on me soon enough.

The only thing she could do was pray...,

"Lord, please let me get out of here alive!"

I know you are over there praying. The last one prayed, too. She sat right there in that same seat, just like you and cried like a baby. But I promise you, she's not crying or praying anymore. And neither will you, pretty soon.

She kept praying to God and trying to figure out a way to escape. Then she remembered that she had a serrated pocketknife in her pocket.

"Lord, I don't know why this is happening! But please help me get out of here alive. Just help me stab him in the eye, then I can run and escape."

He finally arrived to the vacant building.

Well, as you can see. Oooops, my bad... I should have said, 'as you can see out of ONE eye'...

She didn't respond. She kept praying in her heart.

What? You don't like my humor? Well, don't worry about it. My own mother didn't like my humor. As a matter of fact, my mother didn't like me at all. But I taught her a lesson or two as well. Look around. What do you see?

SLAP! *Don't ignore me. Answer me when I am talking to you! And if I give you instructions, follow them. Now, what do you see?*

She squeezes the tears from her eyes and looks around.

"I see a building."

That's right! A building. This is a huge building, little girl, over 5,000, maybe even 6,000 feet, all the way around, on every side. And the back side of it is facing a wooded area. It's dead back there, little girl. No life at all. Nobody can help you now. This whole area is a mile all the way around. It has been shut down for years. Look at this street. There are no streetlights. They are all broken out. No businesses are anywhere close. There are no cars running through here, no bus stops. Nothing. The only thing out here, little girl, is you and me and this big surprise I can't wait to give you once we get inside this vacant building, he said while massaging the big surprise. He rolled down his window and stuck his head out.

182

There's always a nice breeze out here this time of night. Can you feel it?

ANSWER ME!

"No, I don't feel it."

INHALES DEEPLY. Aaaahhhhhh! I love doing that! Makes me feel free every time.

Whining quietly.

Didn't we just have this conversation? NO TALKING! All that whining! I like my girls pretty. Now, dry that pretty little face.

SNOT, TEARS, AND BLOOD STREAK ACROSS PRETTY LITTLE FACE.

See, now you are pretty again... well, except for that ugly eye. How did that happen anyway? LAUGHS.

MASSAGING SURPRISE AGAIN.

WHOLE BODY JERKS.

RUBS DEFLATED SURPRISE.

Now, here is what I want you to do. I want you to scream out of this window as loud as you can and say, 'Hello, is anybody out there? Help me. I'm out here all alone, and I am afraid that the bad man is going to hurt me. Hello! I'm a little girl, and I have been kidnapped. Help me!'

Whining quietly.

ANOTHER BACKHAND TO THE FACE... same eye bleeds again.

SAY IT AGAIN! AGAIN! AGAIN!

SAY IT ONE MORE TIME.

"I can't. My voice is gone."

PERFECT...

You girls are so dumb. Works every time. Now, here's how it's going to go. I'm going to come around and let you out. If you try to run, I will catch you, snap your neck, then kill you after you are dead. If you even try to yell, I will snap your neck. Do you understand?

"Yes." Still praying in her heart.

Momma continued with the story, "When he came around and opened the door, she lunged out at his face and aimed at his eyes with the serrated blade but missed. She stabbed him in the face twice and in the arm, twice."

"Mmmm, so that explains the keloids on his face and arms. Got it. What happens next, Momma?"

"He laughs, then snatches that poor girl from the car and wrangles her tiny body like a young Gazelle captured by a pack of wild dogs. He punched her in the face, broke her nose and split open her lips. But she was still swinging both her tiny fists. He laughed more and almost began moaning. But she remained focused and continued fighting, kicking, and screaming. *You got balls, little girl. But you should save your appetite. I'll be serving dessert in a minute.* Still, she continued fighting for her life, but was no more a threat to her formidable opponent than a mouse caught in a viper's fangs. His dark eyes lit up, and his venomous fangs became a butcher's stainless-steel blades. He was salivating like that pack of wild dogs ready to devour his delicate prey. He took the knife from her swinging hands and slowly slid it down her smooth, supple face."

184

At that point, Momma's knees began to buckle. I grabbed her and held her tight, so she wouldn't hit the ground.

"I got you, Momma. It's ok. It's ok, baby. I got you."

Momma whispered lifelessly... "She was the prettiest girl in the whole school, and he ruined her. He cut her from her forehead all the way down to her chin or neck. He was known for that kind of thing. He even followed a girl home from a party one night and raped her and never did leave her house. He just took over her apartment like it was his. He is a terrible man. He defecates on everything he touches. GET ME OUT OF HERE!"

Tears began welling in my eyes. I kept thinking, "This can't be true. No, no, no..."

Momma pulled away from me, and turned the bottle up, and drank another ¼. "Then he raped that poor girl."

I couldn't believe what I was hearing. Rage and sorrow were swimming around in my head. My blood was beginning to boil. I could hear the devil talking to me. My head began to pound.

"After he raped her," Momma said, "he stabbed her in the stomach and left her for dead. He even set her hair on fire. Then he disappeared. This is the first time that I have seen him. That was at least 18 or 19 years ago. Maybe even 20. How did he end up here? That happened over a thousand miles away from here. How could me and that monster end back up in the same place?"

"Do you remember her name, Momma?"

No, I don't remember her name. But I do remember that it started with an "A." It was a really pretty name. It was different. She was the only girl around with that name at the time. Something like Avalon, Avalia, Avalanche, or something."

"Was it Avia?"

"Could have been. Sounds familiar. But I really don't remember."

Momma turned up the Henney and finished it, then turned and began walking away from the corner.

"Man, Ace," Bluff said. "She left her cases."

"Don't worry about it, bro. Donate them to the guys."

I could barely keep my feet on the ground. This strange woman's words flung open the curtains of my futile fascination against my mother and unfolded a fundamentally foolish foundation upon which I fixed all my fury.

It was flawed.

Feeble.

My truth was as feeble as a floundering fool.

It was unfounded,

Flimsy,

Fragile,

Flimflammy,

Flexible,

Infeasible,

Fanciful,

Frivolous,

Factless.

Why couldn't I see it?

Ray Charles saw it.

So did five boys from Mississippi.

It's been brazenly boasting in plain sight all these years.

But I was blind.

My frail fallacies fell down on the floor,

Like warm fluid pouring from my eyes,

Emulsifying my fallacies,

Revealing a fractured truth.

I was blindsided by falsehoods,

Fooled by feverish feelings,

And fables,

And fabrications,

And fumblings,
And fraudulence,
And findings,
And fibbings,
And factualizing fictions.
And that's the truth,
That's the hardcore, hard-hitting truth.
No more shutters.
Now I have nothing to be mad at Momma about.
All I have is her truth.
And my lie.
My lie is naked,
Exposed,
Raw
Bloody meat.
Ferocious,
Deflowered,
Manhandled,
Fondled,
Given the middle finger,
FLIPPED,
DEFACED,
DISFIGURED.
I get it now.
My truth is an hourglass,
Punch at a party,
An offer I can't refuse,
It's too good to be true.
My truth is dead,
Dead wrong,
A one-night stand,

A lie,
A hoax.
My truth tricked me,
Deceived Me,
Ditched me.
My truth fathered me.
Momma's truth mothered me.
Momma... I'm sorry!

"Ace, man. What's up?" Bluff said. "Did I miss something?"

"Bluff, take me home. Take me home."

"No problem, bro. Let's go." While walking to the car, Bluff called Gap from his cell phone. "Look, man. I need you. Borrow Dad's car, and meet me at Ace's mom's house. We will be there in 30 minutes."

"Got it, bro. Out." Gap's voice emitted from the phone speaker.

Everything kept playing back in my head.

Lord, I've never prayed before, but PLEASE, LET ME BE WRONG. Please tell me that I am wrong. This can't be real! This can't be happening.

The tears dropped from my eyes like enemy missiles dropping from the sky. Thoughts of killing that fool and thoughts of getting to Momma collided. I couldn't decide if the pain of what he did to Momma, or the pain of what I did to her was worse. But one thing was sure, I was going to kill that fool tonight. I knew he was foul.

When we pulled up to the house, Gap was already parked outside. Bluff barely had time to put the car into park before I grabbed the keys and rushed toward the front door.

Bluff and Gap were right behind me.

My hands were shaking uncontrollably, and the missiles continued shooting from my eyes.

"Here, give me the keys, bro. Let me open it. I got you," Gap said.

Once Gap opened the door, I didn't have to go far. Momma was right there in the living room asleep in her favorite Lazy-boy recliner.

I ran over to her and fell on my knees and laid my head in her lap.

"Momma. I'm so sorry. I'm sorry for the way I have treated you all these years. I have been such a terrible son. Please forgive me, Momma. I know what happened to you. I understand. I had everything wrong. You were right. I love you, Momma. I'm sorry.

"Everything you did was for me. You are not a liar. You are a loving mother who was trying to protect her son. I get that now. I met this lady today, she dates Gap and Bluff's dad. She told me everything. Is it true, Momma? Is it true? Are you the girl she was talking about? Was it you, Momma? Was it you?"

Gap and Bluff looked at one another intensely. Gap was confused. Bluff hunched his shoulders...

"Momma... please tell me that I have it wrong. Please tell me that what I am thinking right now is incorrect. I KNOW THIS FOOL DIDN'T HURT YOU LIKE THAT! I KNOW HE DIDN'T! I am so sorry, Momma. Please forgive me."

Momma didn't answer.

I was so busy trying to make things right and apologize for all the wrong that I had done, that I did not realize that Momma was dead.

Momma died in her sleep.
She died in her favorite chair,
Her Lazy Boy Recliner.
An onslaught of thoughts flooded my mind.
WHY? rang the loudest.
Then *NO!...*
No, she can't be gone.
Come back Momma, don't go!
But it was too late. Momma was already gone. I killed her.
She died of a broken heart.
That last argument killed her.
I DIDN'T GET A CHANCE TO SAY I'M SORRY!
I DIDN'T SAY GOODBYE!
MOMMMA!!!
Lord, please don't take my momma from me. I was Momma's song. Now, I know why she sang it all the time. Why Lord? WHY? It should have been me. It should have been me.

"Bluff, I'm hurting, man. All these years, I disrespected and disowned my mother. I rained on her like she was nothing, like she was one of these fools out there in the street, bro. And all she wanted to do was protect me. She didn't want me to feel bad about how I came into this world.

"You know, every morning, I wake up furious. I wanted to hurt someone, damage something, somebody, anybody. I always thought it was the devil, but now I believe it was him. That bad part of me. That bad part of my DNA, bro. My mom was trying to protect me from that. But I didn't let her. I despised her. I did the opposite of everything she taught me. She said treat other people with respect. I was disrespectful every day of my life. That's the real reason those teachers didn't like me, man. Gap, you know I came reckless. You used to talk to me at that school and try to get me to calm down. I had to graduate early, or I would have gotten kicked out eventually for going in on those fools. I was mad for nothing, bro. It was like I had a split personality. I couldn't help myself. That's why Momma was so patient with me, bro. She loved me and worked with me. But I was foul, bro. She told me to never put my hands on a female...

"That's why me and Shaquita broke up, bro. I didn't quit her. She quit me. I was reckless, and she had too much pride and respect for herself to allow me to rain down on her. She cut me off and didn't look back, but she was an adult about it. She told me to grow up. Next thing I know, I was surrounded by her brothers, bro. The girl wasn't nothin' nice.

"You were right, Momma. You were right. I was wrong all this time. How could I have been so blind, bro? How? You and Gap tried to tell me. I can't even be mad at her if she would have put me out or called the police on me. Man! I put hands on my own mother. I'M SORRY!"

I stood to my feet, looked down at my waist, and a floodgate of tears erupted from my eyes all over again. I took the belt off and turned the buckle over and read the inscription again. "Aaron is a Hebrew word meaning High

Mountain, Mountain of Strength, Exalted, Enlightened, and Bearer of Martyrs."

I turned to Bluff. He was standing there speechless, with a stream of tears running down his face.

"See, man. Momma loved me. Now I know why she always told me it was a one-night stand. Now I know why she didn't tell me about my father. Despite how I arrived, she had nothing but love for me."

I gazed at my belt again while wiping the tears from my eyes so that I could read it to both of them. I read it over and over… "Aaron is a Hebrew word meaning High Mountain, Mountain of Strength, Exalted, Enlightened, and Bearer of Martyrs."

Momma, I get it now.

I looked up toward the sky, toward God, and sang like I never sang before.

Tears were streaming down all our faces.

Every painful word had a life of its own, a purpose, a cause, a restorative work to do. Momma was on a mission. Her purpose was single. Every pause, every high, and every low was all by design. All of it made me reflect, reminisce, regret, and repent.

Now, I understand why Momma had so much passion and will and determination and anger and sorrow and terror and love and sweetness and bitterness when she sang. Momma's song was necessary. It was ugly and beautiful. Right and wrong. Painful and calming, all at the same time.

She'd close her eyes tightly, and rock back and forth in her recliner, and let the tears fall, then push the words out. Sometimes they fell out with ease. Other times she had to go in and dig them out. Other times they crawled. Sometimes they had a limp, just like Momma's limp.

I let the tears fall just like Momma. My voice quivered, and rocked and trembled, and quaked just as hers. I stayed off-key, just like Momma did. I could feel the grieving bravado thundering in my mourning throat. I grimaced, and groaned, and wept, and creaked, and clenched. Momma didn't do those things. But I sure did. I wasn't strong like her. I wailed and whimpered and squealed and whined and wheezed.

Momma sang with hope.

I sang with regret.

She sang with emotion.

My emotions were not in a good place:

Frustration,

Sorrow,

Remorse,

Revenge,

Dispathy.

Lord, don't move my mountain,
But give me the strength to climb,
(Bereaving, tearfully...)
And Lord, don't take away my stumbling blocks,
But lead me all around

(Weeping deeply...)
Lord, I don't bother nobody,
I try to treat everybody the same,
But every time I turn my back
They scandalize my name

(Bawling my eyes out. Lord, I did Momma so
wrong. She was singing about me... Crying deeply
– the way I used to hear Momma cry...)
But oh Jesus,
You don't have to move my mountain,
But give me the strength to climb,
And Lord don't take away my stumbling blocks,
But lead me all around,
(Wailing uncontrollably...)

Bluff steps up to hug me, but Gap stops him.
"Don't hug him, bro. Let him get it out. He's been on that
path about his mother a long time. He needs to free
himself. Let him have this."
Bluff concedes and steps back.
God, you answered Momma's prayer. You didn't
take away her stumbling block. But instead, you took her
away. And now she's gone. Mommaaaaa! Lord, I'm sorry.
I tormented Momma. I made her a prisoner in her own
home. I was a terrible son. She was a good mother, God. I
always knew it. I was just so mean and evil, like him...
"I USED TO HIT MY MOMMA, BLUFF.
I PUNCHED HER, MAN!
I PUNCHED HER ALL THE TIME,
AND SHE NEVER RETALIATED!
I KICKED HER AND TRIPPED HER AND SHOVED
HER AROUND! I EVEN SPIT IN HER FACE! I USED
TO SLAP MOMMA AND CALL HER LITTLE GIRL! I
TREATED HER LIKE SHE WAS A CHILD!

I TREATED HER LIKE THAT MONSTER TREATED
HER AND SHE CONTINUED LOVING ME! I'M SO
ASHAMED. I SHOULD BE DEAD. NOT HER! BRING
HER BACK AND TAKE ME! PLEASEEEE!
I'M SORRY, GOD!
I'M SORRY!
HELP ME GOD!
I AM NOTHING LIKE HIM!
I CAN'T BE. I DON'T WANT TO BE LIKE HIM!
I REFUSE TO BE LIKE HIM!
I'M LIKE MY MOMMA!
GOD, I'M LIKE MY MOMMA!
SHE RAISED ME. NOT HIM!
I'M NOTHING LIKE HIM!
I DON'T WANT TO BE LIKE HIM,
HURTING PEOPLE JUST BECAUSE I CAN!
HELP ME CHANGE, GOD!
THAT MONSTER RAPED MY MOTHER!
HE RAPED HER!
THAT'S WHY SHE WAS DISFIGURED!
HE BUTCHERED HER FACE!
MOMMA WAS BEAUTIFUL, BLUFF!
SHE WAS BEAUTIFUL, MAN!
AND SHE TRIED TO FIGHT BACK!
MOMMA WAS STRONG, BLUFF!"

Tears of both pain and admiration stormed my
face. I was angry and proud all at the same time. I was out
of my mind. I am going to kill that monster!

"SHE WAS STRONG, BLUFF, MAN!
SHE STABBED HIM IN HIS FACE
AND IN HIS ARMS!

SHE DIDN'T GIVE UP!
MOMMA WASN'T WEAK AT ALL!
HE WAS JUST TOO STRONG!
THE ODDS WERE AGAINST HER!
HE WAS A GIANT COMPARED TO HER.
WHY DIDN'T SHE DIE?
BECAUSE OF ME, MAN!
MOMMA FOUGHT FOR HER LIFE FOR ME!
GOD, YOU LOOKED OUT FOR MOMMA.
AND YOU KEPT HER ALIVE, JUST FOR ME!
ALL THESE YEARS, BLUFF,
I HAVE BEEN JUDGING HER,
CALLING HER ALL KINDS OF NAMES.
SHE DIDN'T DESERVE ANY OF IT, BLUFF!
SHE DIDN'T DESERVE ANY OF IT,
BUT SHE FOUGHT BACK,
SHE FOUGHT FOR ME!
SHE WAS JUST A LITTLE GIRL,
BLUFF, SHE WAS JUST 15 YEARS OLD!
SHE WAS A CHILD!
SHE WAS A VIRGIN!
AND SHE DIDN'T ABORT ME, BLUFF!
HE STABBED HER IN HER STOMACH~
WHY DIDN'T SHE DIE?
WHY DID I LIVE?
HE TRIED TO KILL ME,
BUT SHE WAS TOO STRONG
TO LET THAT HAPPEN!
I KNOW SHE WAS PRAYING, BLUFF, MAN,
AND I KNOW HER FAITH KEPT HER ALIVE!
GOD IS REAL!

I HAD IT ALL WRONG!
I WAS WRONG ABOUT EVERYTHING!
ALL THESE YEARS I THOUGHT GOD WAS JUST IN
MOMMA'S HEAD. BUT HE'S REAL, BRO!
I FEEL HIM NOW!
SOMETHING IS HAPPENING TO ME, BRO!
I can really feel God moving on me, bro!
Look at me, man. I'm shaking!
I held out both my hands. Both were shaking.
MOMMA IS A MIRACLE!
SHE LIVED, SO I COULD LIVE!
SHE ASKED GOD FOR THE STRENGTH TO CLIMB
HER MOUNTAIN,
AND THEN SHE HAD ME,
AND LOVED ME,
EVEN WHEN I DIDN'T LOVE HER BACK!
SHE CARED FOR ME,
AND TREATED ME LIKE HER LITTLE KING!"

Momma never treated me poorly. She prayed to God and asked Him to bless her mind to see me and not the situation. She did not regard what happened to her. Momma realized that what happened to her did not define who she was. In spite of this thing, Momma remained sweet and kind and loving. Momma loved me. Momma did not live her life, or make her decisions based upon that one horrible, horrible incident. She separated herself from that experience, and I know it hurt her until the day she died.

I remember hearing Momma crying in the bathroom. I could hear her wail over the shower or running bathwater. Sometimes she would become silent, then wail all over again. Now I understand why.

I know it hurt her to see her body, to look upon her nakedness, to see herself unclothed, SCARRED, DEBAUCHED, RUINED.

"That's why she never married, bro.

He stole her youth.

I REMEMBER WHEN I WAS LITTLE,

SHE BOUGHT ME A KING'S CAPE AND SCEPTER.

SHE TOLD ME THAT ONE DAY I WOULD BE A KING

AND THAT I SHOULD RULE IN HONOR.

HOW COULD SHE DO THAT?

KNOWING WHERE I CAME FROM,

AND WHO I CAME FROM,

HOW COULD SHE LOVE ME, BLUFF?

I WOULDN'T BLAME HER IF SHE HADN'T KEPT ME.

HOW COULD I?

I KNEW THERE WAS SOMETHING ABOUT THAT

PUNK. I COULD SEE IT IN HIS EYES.

I COULD SEE IT IN HIS EYES."

"Who is he talking about," Gap asked Bluff.

"He met his father today bro, and it's not good."

"Wow! Well, I'm down with whatever" Gap said.

My fury was full blaze. **"COME ON, BLUFF, MAN, Y'ALL, LET'S GO!!!** Let's go get this punk! He no longer has breathing privileges!"

Uncontrollably, I screamed in the air the same thing over and over.

"I'M COMING FOR YOU, YOU HEAR ME? I'M COMING FOR YOU!"

Bluff reached out and grabbed me. I was a wild boar, but he wouldn't let me go.

"LET ME GO, BLUFF! LET ME GO! I GOTTA GO SNUFF THIS FOOL OUT! I'MMA KILL HIM, BLUFF! I'MMA KILL HIM! HE DEAD! GET THE HEAT! HE DEAD! HE DEAD!!!"

"That's not you, Ace! That's not you. That's not what Momma wanted for you, Ace. It's not. She wanted so much more for you, Ace. That's why she kept you and loved you. She loves you, Ace. That will never change."

"I KNOW, I KNOW... BUT I HATE THIS FOOL! I NEED TO FINISH THIS, BRO. IT'S BECAUSE OF HIM THAT I AM SO MESSED UP. LET ME GO."

I began trying to wrestle away from Bluff again, but he had me in a vice grip. He continued gripping me until he felt my anger subsiding. I felt like a little boy in his father's arms.

"Why did he have to be my daddy, Bluff. Out of all the men and riffraff in the world, I had to have a scuzz-bucket as my father. I'mma kill that fool, Bluff. I got to."

Amid all my pain, I failed to see that Momma had gotten my gift from off the TV and opened it.

She was laid back in her Lazy Boy, wearing the dress that I bought her. She was looking so beautiful and peaceful. The dress was form-fitting. I could see the lopsidedness in her stomach.

"That's why she always wore those big baggy dresses, Bluff. Her stomach did not heal evenly from the stab wounds."

Her left side was at least 4 or 5 inches larger than her right. I touched it with my hand, it was hard and

bumpy. I rubbed it gently. "I love you, Momma. I love you. You are so beautiful. I am so sorry."

I removed my hand from her stomach and gently placed it upon her face. That's when I noticed the wig. She was wearing the wig that I purchased for her. It was the same style she wore in the picture on her dresser in her room. Her headwrap was on the floor next to her recliner.

"Momma, I am sorry for the way I treated you. I was so wrong about everything. Your smocks and headdresses were beautiful. I was out of line. Please forgive me, Momma."

I reached down next to the recliner and lifted the headdress from the floor. "I'm sorry for trying to change you. I was too blind to see the perfectly perfect beautiful person that you are. You were right before my eyes, and I did not see."

My heart skipped a beat when I removed the wig from Momma to replace it with her headwrap. Her entire scalp was scarred. He torched her. He torched her alive. And now I understand why her hands were so rough. She was a burn victim. She put the fire out with her hands.

Even through all the heavy tears blinding my eyes, I could see that smug punk out there lying through his teeth. I wanted to run out of the house and do him in right where he stood, but I couldn't pull myself away from Momma.

Momma was almost completely bald. She had patches of hair and patches of alopecia. He ruined her hair. Much of her scalp was destroyed down to her hair follicles. Her scalp did not heal well. It was permanently disfigured. It was larger than what suited her body. The headwraps camouflaged the size. She appeared to wear a bulky headdress, but it was, in fact, a very thin, lightweight piece of cloth. All of the bulkiness was the thick layers of scar tissue that formed on her scalp because of the burns she sustained.

I collapsed to the floor and fell to my knees.

"IF IT'S THE LAST THING I DO, BLUFF, I AM GOING TO KILL THAT CLOWN."

Coughing, softly...

Bluff and I look at one another.

"Momma! Momma!"

More soft coughing...

Momma struggles to open her eyes.

I have never been so happy to see that little face squinting in all my life.

I started laughing and praised God.

"Thank you, Jesus! Thank you, God! Bluff, go in the kitchen and get me a bottle of water. Get one from the pantry. She can't drink ice-cold water. Her stomach is too sensitive. Now, I understand why. Even through all her pain and scars, she was always thinking about me. I couldn't see, Gap. I couldn't see her pain, man. I was blind to it all.

"She was strong, Gap. All these years, these scars were hidden in plain sight. It's like they were invisible. Her pain was invisible. She hid it all from me just so I would not have to have any pain, man. This hurts, man. It hurts."

"Here, Momma." I untwisted the cap and placed the bottle up to her lips."

"What are you talking about, baby? Who are you planning on hurting?"

"Momma, I thought you were gone."

"Gone, gone where, son? As you can see, I'm right here."

"But I thought you were..."

"Not yet, son. Not yet. Sometimes I get those real bad headaches and can't do anything. I took a couple sleeping pills to help me rest. And boy, I sure feel better. Still a little groggy, but the headache is gone."

Bluff and I look at one another and simultaneously grabbed our chests and smiled.

I reached out and grabbed Momma.

"I love you, Momma. I love you, Momma. I love you." I kissed her all over her face, head, cheeks, eyes, scars, and wounds. The tears would not stop, and neither would my kisses. I told her everything that I had just learned about what happened to her.

I fell on my knees again. "Momma, I am so sorry for all the pain I have caused you. I will never disrespect you again. From this day forward, Momma, I will love and honor you more than you ever can imagine. I could have never been more wrong about anyone than I have been about you, Momma. Please forgive me, Momma. I'm sorry."

All Momma had to say was, "Oh, child, hush."

We hugged and cried and laughed for at least an hour. Bluff had just as much joy as I did, and I think he got in as many hugs as I did as well.

Momma had never felt so loved in all her life. She turned to me with the sternest face she had ever made, "Now, concerning this business of yours... Let that go, Aaron. Let it go, baby. Holding grudges and trying to get revenge on people only makes things worse. Nothing you do will turn back the hands of time and undo what has been done to me. Besides, what if I would have spent the last 18 years trying to get revenge? I would not have been a proper mother to you. Why waste my time doing something that has no good end, when I can spend it on someone who is worthy of my time? You are definitely worth my time, son. I don't regret a day or minute of having you. You are the very source of my joy. Without you in my life, it would have been completely empty. I was beholding to you, son. I knew I had lots of hard work ahead of me, but The Lord always told me to hold on and not give up. He let me know that it was MY blood running through your veins. Blood is not just about DNA, son. It's also about environment and what an individual is exposed to. It's about what they see, what they learn, what they are taught. I taught you to be a good, gracious, law-abiding man. Now, your choices are yours, but the knowledge that you have is bigger than your choices. Choices are simply what you decide to do. Knowledge dictates what you should do. You are my son, Aaron. Mine. And I know you will make the right decision, regardless of how you feel right now. They say cream always rises to the top. I kinda see the best in you rising to the top, son. I have no doubts about it."

"Momma, you are right, and as I said, I will never disrespect you again. But as a man and as your son, I feel like I need to do this. That low-down, grimy person does not deserve to have air in his lungs. He does not have the right to be sucking in oxygen. He hasn't earned no oxygen, Momma! He tried to take your oxygen. I'mma do to him

what he tried to do to you. I'm sure he will understand that."

"She's right, Ace," Bluff said. "Your mother is right. Everything is coming full circle."

"Ace," Momma said, "Go on in there and get yourself and your friends something to eat. I have all that chicken and rice from last night. It's enough for everyone. I'm glad I cooked extra, I know how you like your chicken and rice."

"That's right Momma, I love chicken and rice, and I love you, too."

Momma didn't say anything, but her smile curled all the way up to her ears. I burst into a joyous laughter. "Before y'all go in there and eat, go over there and get my remote, honey. Turn the TV on, it's time for the 5 o'clock news. Put it on channel three. I like the news on that channel. They are not bias like some of these news channels can be."

"No problem, Momma, I'll turn it to any channel you want. I got you, darling!" I turned to channel three and all our mouths flung open. A slow chill ran up and down my spine as I read the headline flashing across the television screen:

MAN SHOT AND KILLED IN BELLO HEIGHTS...

"New Momma," shot and killed the new guy right after we left. As the news report continued, it was stated that she fired three shots. Two were to his boastful, proud chest, with not so much as a swerve in the wind. They landed one right after the other, directly into his cold, blackened heart. The third was poignant and just as deliberate. It landed uncompromisingly... squarely into

206

the center of his unsuspecting, well deserving head. His brains flew out the back of his head and scattered like ashes into the air and on the ground near the ice chest upon which he sat. His shocked body stiffened liked a hardened corpse instantly, then fell over backwards and hit the ground like a useless block of ice.

New Momma alleged he raped her 25 years ago and ruined her life. Through her tears she yelled, "I WASN'T THE ONLY ONE. IT'S TIME FOR HIM TO PAY! IT'S TIME. EVEN IF I SPEND THE REST OF MY LIFE BEHIND PRISON BARS, I WILL BE AT PEACE, KNOWING THAT HE GOT WHAT WAS COMING TO HIM. HE IS FINALLY OFF THE STREET AND WILL NEVER BE ABLE TO HURT ANYONE ELSE THE WAY HE HURT ME AND RUINED MY LIFE!"

The police then gently put her in handcuffs and ushered her to the awaiting squad car with flashing lights. The camera turned back to the new guy. He was still on the ground next to the ice chest, dead, in a pool of his own blood and scattered brains.

Momma closed her eyes, then peacefully laid back in her favorite recliner and begin softly singing her song.

"LORD, DON'T MOVE MY MOUNTAIN."

A Note from The Author

Teresa Collins

Educator, Influencer, B.A. Psychology

THE SONG HIS MOTHER SINGS

Parent Abuse

The Song His Mother Sings addresses the issue of parent abuse to bring awareness to it and guidance on how to overcome it. This story is not a diagnosis of parent abuse, nor is it an informational pamphlet that offers tactical solutions. It is a story that reflects the reality of parent abuse in the lives of many families across the globe. It is a magnifying glass that focuses on this aspect of society. It is a means to bring awareness to this problem which will uncover the cause and ultimately lead to solutions.

Sadly, parents who are trapped in the painful cycle of parent abuse struggle with finding the courage to take the necessary steps to overcome it. They feel shame because they do not want anyone to know that they are afraid of their own child. They feel guilty because they blame themselves for their child's poor behavior. Sometimes parents fear the guilt they will feel if they turn their child over to the police. They blame themselves because of past or current parenting failures. Finally, many parents suffer from pride – the need to portray their family as the picture-perfect paradigm of a socially acceptable family unit. They prefer to suffer in silence before exposing such an embarrassing reality. Ironically, the truth is that all families have some form of dysfunction, and parent abuse is terribly common.

What is Parent Abuse?

Parent abuse is a pervasive, yet little known, aspect of domestic violence in global society. Parent abuse is a form of domestic violence in which a person's children (usually juveniles) practice a pattern of behaviors used to maintain power and control over them. Parent abuse is indiscriminatory. All people of all backgrounds, regardless of race, age, gender, or economic status can be a victim or victimizer. Indicative behaviors of parent abuse include physical harm, intimidation, manipulation or control tactics, or other forms of force to cause parents to behave in ways they don't want to – including physical violence, threats, emotional abuse, or financial control.

What Are the Signs of Parent Abuse?

Parent abuse comes with some key warning signs. Some may be subtle; others may be blatant. If you detect any of the following behaviors from your child, take immediate action.

1. **Feeling Intimidated by Your Child.** Intimidation is a way of frightening a parent into doing something they do not want to do. Juveniles use harsh words, tones, and even glares to intimidate their parents. Although testing boundaries is normal for children, it is NOT NORMAL for a parent to fear their child or feel threatened with vindictive retaliation.

2. **Oppositional Defiance.** Oppositional defiance is when a child displays no respect for a parent's authority, rules, or person. It may be common for children to display some level of defiance as they mature, but it is a serious problem when a child

has a daily pattern of defiance with no fear or concern of consequences.

3. **Increasingly Violent Tendencies.** Increasingly violent tendencies is a child's pattern of violent behavior that continues to escalate to the point of destroying property and harming people. Some indicators include punching furniture, aggressively pushing people, throwing things at or toward a parent, threatening violence, or physically assaulting parents. Abusive behavior is not a phase of childhood or adolescence. It is a dangerous sign of abuse and needs to be addressed immediately.

How to Address Parent Abuse

Although parent abuse can feel crippling, there is a way out. If you identify parent abuse in your life, consider taking the following steps to overcome it.

1. **Set Boundaries & Consequences and Communicate Them.** Ensure that your child understands your boundaries. In a conversation with your child, communicate which behaviors are acceptable and which behaviors are not. Be clear about how you expect to be addressed and physically handled. Your actions must support your verbal boundaries by immediately addressing violations of your set boundaries. You can address boundary violations by clearly communicating consequences for violating your personal boundaries. You must enforce your consequences. Never make idle threats. List clear

reactions to your child's behaviors and follow through. Neglecting to follow through with clear consequences to boundary violations will reinforce to your child their ability to disregard your boundaries and authority.

2. **Contact the Police.** If your child is behaving violently toward you, eventually their actions can become critical and even fatal. If you have lost control of your child, you must contact local law enforcement who are equipped to support you and give your child the services they need. Although you may be reluctant to involve the police in situations concerning your child, you will be harming your child if you allow them to engage in violent behavior without consequences. Involving the police protects your safety and your child's.

3. **Find Someone to Help You.** Parent abuse is a silent pandemic. It may be difficult but speak up! Call relatives, friends, acquaintances or anyone who can support you as you strive to free yourself from parent abuse. If you feel that it will be counterproductive to involve people who are close to you, take advantage of local domestic violence hotlines, family counselors, or support groups. The resources are readily available. You are not alone. You do not have to suffer alone. Do not let parent abuse prevail. Take the steps necessary to save yourself and your child.

The National Hotline can be accessed via the nationwide number 1–800–799–SAFE(7233) or TTY 1–800–787–3224 or (206) 518-9361 (Video Phone Only for Deaf Callers).

The Hotline provides service referrals to agencies in all 50 states, Puerto Rico, Guam and the U.S. Virgin Islands.   Persons can also contact the Hotline through an email request from the Hotline website Visit disclaimer page .

Services are provided without regard to race, color, national origin, religion, gender, age, or disability (including deaf and hard of hearing). Assistance is available in English and Spanish with access to more than 170 languages through telephonic interpreter services. https://www.acf.hhs.gov/fysb/programs/family-violence-prevention-services/programs/ndvh

www.ingramcontent.com/pod-product-compliance
Lightning Source LLC
Chambersburg PA
CBHW051131020726
47501CB00005B/1448

* 9 7 8 1 7 3 7 0 0 2 5 0 5 *